SUITCASE GIRL

SUITCASE GIRL TRILOGY BOOK ONE (ABBY KANE
FBI THRILLER #7)

TY HUTCHINSON

CHAPTER ONE

A MISTY DRIZZLE fell throughout the day and continued into the night, leaving the dockworkers at the Port of Oakland longing to punch out of their shift. Further compounding working conditions, a fog had begun to roll in, cutting down on visibility.

The stevedore in charge rallied his men, urging them to remain steadfast in their duties, as they unloaded the last cargo ship on the work order.

Up above, about fifty feet, a container crane held a shipping container in its iron grip and was in the process of lowering it to a waiting forklift. The container touched down with a thunk, and a couple of longshoremen quickly unhooked the four cables securing the container to the spreader. One gave the operator of the crane a thumbs-up.

"Last one and we're out," the stevedore shouted to the forklift operator.

"Ain't that the truth. I got it from here."

"You sure?" the stevedore asked as he removed his gloves.

"Yeah, I'm good. Go home."

The forklift operator pushed the lever controlling the mast and lifted the container exactly five feet from the pavement. He backed up, spun the vehicle around, and drove in the opposite direction of where the other workers were heading.

Reflective yellow dock lines led the way to a remote area where there were no personnel—just containers stacked four high.

He eased the forty-foot-long container into an area shielded from the dock lights and lowered the mast. The container again thunked as it connected with the pavement. He backed the lift truck away and then shut the engine off before sending a text message on his cell phone.

Carlos Medina had worked at the shipyard for fifteen years. While he had gotten used to the daily grind, he hated being there longer than needed. The men he worked with were the last scheduled crew on the docks that night, but Medina had some unfinished business he needed to take care of before heading home.

Medina sat quietly, listening to a distant siren cry out—it wouldn't be Oakland if there weren't any. He clasped his hands together and rubbed vigorously until he felt the burn. He was anxious to put something warm in his stomach; the leftover chili he had at home in the fridge would do fine.

He checked his watch again. *What's taking so long?*

Just then his phone chimed.

"Finally," he muttered as he read the text message.

Ten minutes later, Medina heard the engines of vehicles approaching. Two black vans came into view with their head-lights off. They came to a stop a few feet away from the forklift, and two individuals exited each one. They always dressed the same when they showed up: black jeans, black hoodies, and Wayfarer sunglasses.

He didn't know their names or what they looked like under their disguises, although he did figure out one of them was a girl.

There was never a discussion. The arrangement stood the same as always. Medina would move the container to a set location, send a text, and wait for their arrival.

He watched as one of them dealt with the lockbox on the container before pulling open the double doors.

Medina never allowed his gaze to linger; he felt it was better to give the impression that he had no interest in what they were removing from the container. Occasionally he took a peek.

He lit a cigarette and ignored the two individuals entering the steel box with flashlights. He could hear them talking, in Chinese—at least that was what it sounded like to him. A little later they would begin unloading their goods from the container.

The shipment was always the same.

One by one the girls exited the container, walking hunched over with their arms crossed over their chests. They were clothed and wore shoes. Some shivered, but that was the extent of any dramatics.

Medina never made it a point to count, but it seemed each shipment contained between eight to twelve girls. This was the third he had been involved with. He took a long pull on his cigarette, and the tip flared a bright red.

The girls were directed toward one of the vehicles where two other individuals waited. One, a man, held a clipboard. His female cohort would shine a small penlight into each girl's face as they looked over paperwork. Satisfied that the girl in front of them matched their list, the female would then help the girl into the rear of the van.

That night the process deviated when the fifth girl approached. After the flashlight check, they had her wait next to them instead of loading her into the van. She, by far, was the smallest of the group. She didn't shiver or cry or fidget. She just stood motionless with her head down.

Not much later the men in the container appeared with the last two girls and escorted them to the van, where they were also checked against the list.

The group then had a brief discussion about the girl who'd been pulled aside. Medina detected English, but he was too far away to make sense of their conversation. A few moments later, the last two girls and the one who had been separated were then loaded into the other van.

One of the men, the tallest, approached Medina and handed him an envelope. Medina always waited until the vehicles drove off before looking inside. The count was never off. Always five thousand dollars in crisp one-hundred notes.

The two vans drove in tandem across the Bay Bridge toward San Francisco. The city skyline twinkled in the night. When they reached the city, they continued to a neighborhood just north of the Tenderloin.

The vehicles parked outside a six-story residential building. For four hours they sat in the vans, waiting for pedestrian and vehicle traffic to die down. By one o'clock it had, and the girls were led quickly into the building.

Two hours later, one of the men exited the building with the girl they had taken extra time with at check-in. They got into the van and drove off. The man made a series of lefts and rights, venturing into the heart of the Tenderloin.

At that time of the morning, the place was barren. It was late enough that even the residents who made their livings on the streets at night had retired, and those who roamed during the day weren't up yet.

The van turned onto a street where a tall building with a concrete plaza in front occupied the entire block. He brought the vehicle to a stop next to the curb and cut the engine. Not a soul, not even a rat marred the silence.

The side door of the van slid open, and the man exited with a suitcase. He looked left and right continuously as he hurried straight toward the entrance of the building, the wheels of the bag bumping along behind him.

When he arrived at the front of the building, he looked around briefly before releasing the suitcase handle and walking away. He never once looked back.

There was nothing special about the suitcase, the dimensions were thirty-one inches by twenty-two by thirteen. Fairly typical. If there were something conspicuous, it would have to be the fact that something inside of the bag shook it.

CHAPTER TWO

The navy blue Crown Victoria came to a stop next to the curb. Detective Pete Sokolov exited the driver's side dressed in a charcoal gray suit. He was a veteran of the San Francisco Police Department, having spent most of his career working at the Central precinct. He stood tall, over six feet, with shoulders broad enough to require that his suits be tailored. He wore his blond hair high and tight.

His partner, Detective Adrian Bennie, exited the vehicle from the front passenger side. He was dressed in a silver-gray suit and didn't have the height or the width associated with Sokolov, but Bennie always wore a smile that pointed to his dimples.

Sokolov adjusted his jacket. "Why are you always smiling?" he asked, his Russian accent still noticeable.

The two had been partners for eight months. Bennie had worked for the Miami Police before moving out west. He was half white, half Cuban and grew up in the city's Little Havana neighborhood. He never did give Sokolov a reason for the move.

"It's a beautiful day," Bennie chimed. "The sun is shining

bright. The air is clean smelling." He took a sip from a small paper cup. "Coffee here is good, almost as good as the café con leche I'm used to back home. All I need to complete the picture is a piece of—"

"Tostada to dip inside," Sokolov said.

"We're finishing each other's sentences. That means we're growing closer."

"Or maybe you talk too much," Sokolov said gruffly as he rounded the front of the vehicle.

"You know what your problem is?"

"No, but you're about to tell me, right?"

The two walked up the steep granite grade that encircled most of the large plaza, the first deterrent to vehicles attempting to enter the area.

"You got a bleak outlook. Maybe it's because you're Russian. I know it's cold as shit back where you're from, so you've developed this hard outer shell. But man, you've been living in the States since you were a kid. Lighten up a little. Enjoy the music of life." Bennie delivered a quick Salsa dance move.

"Yeah, you're right. I'll start first thing tomorrow morning."

Bennie drained the last of his coffee and tossed the paper cup into a trash receptacle as they passed through a line of security bollards, the second deterrent for vehicles.

The two detectives stopped just outside the large, rectangular glass enclosure that made up the entrance of the Phillip Burton Federal Building. Both had their jackets unbuttoned and their hands resting on their hips.

"Where's the body?" Bennie asked as he spun in a circle.

Sokolov started walking toward the entrance. "Good question," he said.

They passed through one of the double glass doors and

came face to face with an electronic security system that was manned by the Homeland Security's Federal Protective Service. The general public was required to walk through a metal detector and have their belongings pass through an x-ray scanner; employees were put through the same security regimen, but they used a separate entrance that required an identification check.

"Officer Chapman," Sokolov called out.

A man wearing a black suit and talking to one of the uniformed officers monitoring the security system spun around. "Detective Sokolov. It's been awhile. To what do I owe the honor of your presence?"

The two shook hands.

"We're here for the body?"

"What body?"

"We got a call that there was a body here."

Chapman crunched his eyebrows and shook his head. "No body. An abandoned girl was discovered outside this morning. Maybe it's a mix-up on your end? You work Homicide, right?"

"As far as I know."

Chapman stuck his hand out toward Bennie. "FPS Officer Max Chapman. I'm in charge of building security."

"Detective Adrian Bennie. My date here is usually better about introducing me to his friends."

The two chuckled as Sokolov continued to ponder the predicament they were in.

"So you're telling me you found a girl out here this morning?"

"Well, one of my guys found her early this morning, before office hours. She was left in a suitcase right over there." He pointed.

Sokolov frowned. "Suitcase?"

"Yeah. He was on one of his rounds when he spotted the suitcase… thought it was a bomb at first and was seconds from calling it in when the damn thing moved. He unzipped it and found a shivering girl inside."

"Any guess how long she was out there?"

"He says he discovered the bag at 3:15 a.m. Not long. I took a look at the footage from the video surveillance outside. It revealed one man leaving the suitcase. The timing coincided with my guy's last round. When he called me, I instructed him to bring her inside and to call SFPD. Nothing screamed out to me that a federal law had been broken, so it falls in your jurisdiction. Anyway, he tried questioning her, but she remained tight-lipped."

"Man, some parents are messed up," Bennie said. "So the girl's okay?"

"As far as I know. I didn't actually see her. SFPD had already arrived on scene and taken her before I got here. I believe they were heading over to Saint Francis Memorial for a routine check-up." Chapman removed his cell phone. "I have the name of the officer in charge. Probably best you follow up with him if you want more answers." He tapped at the screen. "Officer Frank Burke. Know him?"

Sokolov nodded.

"If there's anything else I can help with, you know how to reach me."

Chapman turned and took two steps when Sokolov stopped him. "You mind if I take a look at that footage, the one with the guy leaving the suitcase?"

"Sure. Follow me."

Chapman led them to an office where FPS personnel were

staring at a bank of monitors.

"You keep a guy in here 24/7?"

"We used to, but... budget cuts. It's only manned during office hours." Chapman had an officer queue the footage.

All four men watched as a man dressed in dark clothing approached with a suitcase. He walked right up to the entrance, dropped the bag, and walked away. It was too dark to make out his facial features.

"That's all you got?" Sokolov asked.

"Yeah. You'll need to subpoena the city for cameras on the street."

"I appreciate your help. Do you know if the officer who took the girl questioned your guy?"

"He took a statement. Everything I told you pretty much encapsulates what he told the officer, but if you want to hear it firsthand, I can arrange for him to be available here. He works the nightshift, so he's off duty now."

"How about his name and address?"

"No problem. Give me a few minutes to pull his records. Oh, and uh, just do me one thing; keep me posted if anything comes of this that involves my guy."

Sokolov and Bennie exited the federal building ten minutes later.

"What are you thinking?" Bennie asked. "We just spent time on something that has nothing to do with us. We investigate dead bodies."

"I know, but the suitcase... it bothers me."

"I would ask if you think there's foul play, but again I'll remind you, there's no body."

Sokolov stopped. He scratched his chin. "Something about this doesn't feel right. If it wasn't for the suitcase, we would have left the second Chapman told us there wasn't a body."

"I hear a 'but' coming."

"I don't buy the child-abandonment theory. Seems off. Unlikely."

"Child abandonment happens all the time, and it doesn't always happen outside of a designated drop-off point like a firehouse. Take the McDonald's incident, for instance."

"Huh?"

"A mother in San Diego took her little boy, a four-year-old, to McDonald's. She ordered him a Happy Meal and then sat him down at a birthday party that was taking place. The boy ate his meal, played the games, had cake and ice cream all before the birthday boy's parents realized they didn't know this kid. The mother was nowhere to be found."

Sokolov grunted as they walked back to their vehicle.

"Look, if you want to spend a little time on this, you know, to make sure this really isn't something other than what it appears to be, it's not a problem."

Sokolov glanced at his watch. "Maybe talking to the girl can help me shake this feeling."

CHAPTER THREE

A WOMAN DRESSED in blue jeans and a floral blouse walked
into the emergency room of Saint Francis Memorial Hospital.
She had chestnut-brown hair that reached the middle of her
back, an olive complexion, and curvy hips.

The rows of seating in the waiting room were already half
filled with people coughing and sniffling and bleeding. She
passed a young man on his cell phone, cradling his arm. "I'm
pretty sure it's broken," she heard him say on her way toward a
nurse sitting behind the reception counter.

"Hi. I'm Christine Rosales." She held her ID card in front of
her. "I'm with Child Protective Services. SFPD brought a
young girl in this morning."

The nurse, a Japanese woman dressed in blue scrubs, looked
up from her paperwork and smiled. "Christine, you know you
don't have to be formal with me."

"I know. I just like to keep you on your toes. How are you
these days?"

"I'm surviving," she said with a heavy breath. "The hubby

and I are taking a cruise next week to Alaska. I'm just counting the days."

"Now that sounds like fun."

"And relaxing," the nurse added.

Rosales motioned behind her with her head. "Looks like it's shaping up to be a busy day."

"It always is," said the nurse. She ran her finger down a manifest. "The girl you're looking for is in exam station six. Go right in."

"Thanks."

Rosales pushed though the swinging double doors and saw a uniformed officer up ahead tapping at his cell phone as he stood next to one of the draped examination rooms.

On her way toward him, she peeked into one of the rooms and saw an unconscious woman lying on a bed with a nurse leaning over her. "Ms. Heath. Can you hear me?" she heard the nurse say.

The officer was too engrossed with his phone to notice Rosales standing in front of him.

"Excuse me. I'm Christine Rosales. I'm with CPS."

The officer looked up. "It's about time. I've been babysitting the kid all morning."

"Traffic," she responded. "Tell me about the girl."

"Standard case of child abandonment. She was found outside the Phillip Burton Building early this morning. She's young, probably between the ages of ten and twelve. No ID and hasn't said a single word. She's been in the examination room for an hour or so. The doc insisted on administering a rape kit."

"Has a missing-persons report been filed?"

"It will be. I'll run her photo through our database of

runaways. But unless the parents come in and claim her, there's not much we can do from here on out."

"That's it?"

"What's to investigate? There's no crime. Child abandonment falls under neglect. This is your agency's responsibility. My guess is she was too much trouble for the parents, and now she'll become a ward of the state, just like all the other abandoned kids."

"Your compassion is overwhelming," she glanced at his badge, "Officer Frank Burke."

"Look, I don't mean to come across that way, but we see this all the time. You know this as much as I do. The world is filled with people who have no business procreating."

Just then the gray curtain was pulled back, revealing a tiny Asian girl dressed in a hospital gown. She sat upright at the edge of the bed with her feet dangling above the floor. A nurse exited the room without saying a word.

Another woman wearing green scrubs with a stethoscope around her neck was busy writing on the girl's chart.

She looked up. Rosales didn't recognize her.

"I'm Dr. Sonya Greer. I'm the attending physician here. Which of you do I talk to about the girl?"

Burke pointed at Rosales. "She's the woman in charge now."

"Hey, wait a minute," Rosales protested.

"My hands are tied here." He began walking away.

"But..."

"Get the girl to talk," he said without looking back. "If anything comes of it, contact us."

The two watched Burke disappear behind the swinging doors.

Christine reached out a hand and Greer shook it. "I'm

Christine Rosales, CPS."

"We'll need another hour or so with the girl," Greer said. "Administering the rape kit takes a while, and then I'm recommending she stay the night for observation."

"And her condition?"

Greer closed the curtain, cutting the girl off from them.

"By all appearances, she's healthy. There are no signs of physical trauma on her body that I can see; nothing to indicate a struggle. If she was abandoned, it seems as though she may not have realized it. Visibly it doesn't look like she was sexually abused, but we'll see what the rape kit reveals. Of course with the backlog at the crime lab, who knows when that'll be. She needs a shower, something to eat, but other than that, she's fine."

"The officer said she hasn't talked?"

"Not a peep."

The nurse who left the examination room earlier returned. She handed the doctor a file.

"The results of her blood work," Greer said. She quickly looked it over while biting her lower lip. "They found traces of propofol. This could explain the lack of struggle, willing to be led wherever, even why she's not talking. Temporary memory loss is a common side effect. Shock could also be hampering her ability to speak."

"How long does it last?"

"It depends on the individual. It can be a few hours or a few days. In either case, she should slowly start to recall things."

"I haven't seen you here before," Rosales said.

Greer smiled. "I'm new. Three weeks now."

"Congratulations. And good luck." Christine winked.

"So I can expect to see you again?"

"You got that right."

"It's been nice meeting you. If there aren't any other questions, I do have other patients to attend to."

"Oh, of course. I understand. Um, is it okay if I go inside and talk to the girl?"

"Sure."

Greer stopped after a few steps. "One more thing. We'll need to bag all of her clothes as part of the rape kit. She'll need something to wear when she's released into your custody."

Rosales nodded. She opened the curtain and stepped inside the small space, essentially a curtain drawn around a bed.

The girl remained sitting in the same position as she last saw her, except this time she was sipping juice from a carton. She kept her head lowered, eyes on the floor as she slurped.

Rosales slouched a little to try to capture the girl's gaze. "Hello. My name is Christine Rosales. What's your name?"

The girl continued to stare at the floor with her vacant eyes. She eventually hit the last of the juice as she sucked air through the straw. Rosales took the carton from her and tossed it into the small trashcan next to the bed.

"Can you tell me where you live or the name of the school you go to?"

Rosales continued her line of questioning, but each one was met with silence.

"It's been that way all morning," the nurse said before she stepped outside the curtain, snapping it shut as she went.

Rosales straightened up. "The doctor wants you to sleep here tonight. Tomorrow morning I'll come back and take you someplace where you'll be more comfortable while we look for your mom and dad."

Rosales placed a hand on the girl's shoulder and gave her a gentle squeeze. "Don't worry. Everything will be okay."

CHAPTER FOUR

Rosales checked her cell phone for messages as she exited the examination area. She had none. She hooked the curled tendrils that framed her face behind her ears as she watched nurses enter and exit examination stations.

The double doors swung open, and a large man, nearly filling the width of the doorway, appeared. He had a determined look on his face. Another suited man followed in his footsteps.

More SFPD?

"Where is examination six?" the man said abruptly to no one in general. A nurse nearby pointed.

Rosales waved the men over to where she stood. "Hi. I'm Christine Rosales. I'm with CPS. Are you here for the abandoned girl?"

"I'm Detective Sokolov. This is Detective Bennie," he said with an accent.

"Are you with missing persons?"

"Homicide."

A crinkle formed between Rosales's eyebrows. "Uh, maybe no one told you, but this girl is alive."

"We heard, there was a mix-up, but we thought we would follow up anyway."

"Oh, well, I'm happy to hear that. The officer who was here earlier said SFPD would be washing their hands of this."

"He's probably right," Sokolov said. "But the suitcase thing bothers me."

"Suitcase? What suitcase?"

"The girl," Bennie said. "She was found stuffed inside of one."

"Really? No one mentioned that to me. The officer gave me the impression she had been left on the front steps with her lunch pail."

"Far from that." Bennie clicked his tongue twice.

"Hmm, that explains the propofol. It showed up in her blood work. Either way, I would appreciate any help from SFPD. I would much rather return her to her parents, if it's possible, than put her into the system."

"Let us talk to the girl. If we hear anything that merits a criminal investigation, we'll get the right people involved."

"Thanks, but a word of warning: she's not a talker." Rosales handed her card to Sokolov. "Keep me posted. I'll be back here tomorrow morning to take her to a shelter."

Sokolov pocketed the card and entered the examination space. "Hmm."

"What is it?" Bennie asked.

"She reminds me of someone," he whispered.

Holding his ID card out to the girl, Sokolov made the introduction. The girl did nothing to acknowledge their presence as she sat on the edge of the bed, kicking her feet back and forth.

"What's your name?" he asked. "Where are your parents? Why were you in the suitcase?"

Bennie placed a hand on his partner's shoulder. "Let me give it a try."

Sokolov moved off to the side. Bennie scrunched down a bit.

"My name is Adrian. Can you tell me your name?"

She continued to stare at the floor.

"It's okay. I know you don't know us. You're probably a little scared right now, but everything will be okay. We're here to help you. We're worried. It's not normal to be inside a suitcase, unless you're playing hide-and-seek. Is that what you were doing? Were you playing a game?"

Nothing but silence. Bennie let out a breath and straightened up. Sokolov removed his cell phone from his pocket. He gently placed two fingers under the girl's chin, raised her head, and took a photo.

"I wonder if she's been printed?" Bennie asked as they headed out of the exam room. "I'll check with Burke. If anything, we can at least make sure she's filed away properly if anyone comes looking for her." Bennie glanced over at his partner, who seemed deep in thought. "I see that look on your face. It's the suitcase, right?"

Sokolov grunted his acknowledgment.

The two detectives emerged from the emergency room and walked back to the Crown Vic.

"You really think there's something here?" Bennie slipped his shades on.

"Usually when a suitcase is involved, it's filled with body *parts*."

"True, but you know what the captain will say about this." Bennie pulled open the passenger door. "We're Homicide."

Sokolov eased his large frame into the driver's seat and

adjusted his jacket. "Maybe someone intended for her to be a homicide."

CHAPTER FIVE

From the moment I woke that morning, I knew it would be a great day. I had slept well—I doubted I'd even moved once. When I washed my face, I noticed the whitehead that had bubbled up on my forehead a few days ago had totally disappeared. Not a hint that it had existed. My abs were looking mighty solid, even though I had skipped more workouts than I preferred in the last few weeks due to work. My hulking, Irish father deserves credit for my fast metabolism. I can thank my Chinese mother for my short stature.

And my hair? Talk about cooperation—straight, silky, and frizz free.

Even the black pantsuit I chose for the day seemed to fit me better than usual. I struck a few poses in front of my standing mirror. *En fuego, Abby. En fuego.*

My steps were light and bouncy as I made my way downstairs. Inside the kitchen, Po Po, my mother in-law, had already started preparing breakfast, but she allowed me to help—a rarity if you know my story.

She was still dressed in her nightgown and shuffled around

wearing her house slippers. We were having the usual: silver-dollar pancakes, bacon, and scrambled eggs.

Ryan, my oldest at eleven, was the first to take a seat at the table. He wore faded jeans and a white polo shirt with the collar popped. His hair was spiked, as usual.

"Load me up. I got a big day ahead of me," he said.

"Oh?" I forked three silver dollars onto his plate.

"Keep 'em coming," he said as he slathered butter onto the cakes.

I added two more to the pile. "Bacon?"

"It's not breakfast without the hog."

"What's gotten into you this morning? You sound like you're gearing up for a cattle run across the Great Plains." I scooped scrambled eggs onto the growing pile of food on his plate.

"Abby." He let out a breath. Yes, he calls me Abby. I came into his life at age four, when I married his father. "Did you forget? As a brown belt, Master Wen is allowing me the chance to help with the training of the younger students at the dojo. He said it will help with my advancement to black belt."

"Of course I remember," I fibbed.

"And Uncle Kyle said he would also train with me more. He said I have a really good chance to get my black belt before I turn twelve."

"I'm very proud of you sweetie." I gave him a kiss on his forehead.

Lucy, my eight-year old, walked in. "What's Ryan done now?"

"Your brother is training students at the dojo."

"Oh, that's nice."

There was a time when Lucy considered her brother to be

God. She followed him everywhere. Agreed with everything he said. Essentially, worshipped the kid. Not anymore.

Lucy had developed her own group of friends and through these friends, I suspect, began paying more attention to herself, especially the clothes she wore. When it came to dressing, she no longer wanted input from me and Po Po.

While I was happy that she was becoming independent, I had to keep an eye on her. Last week she tried to walk out the door wearing white cowboy boots, a jeans skirt, and a *Flashdance*-like T-shirt, complete with revealing rips.

Her reasoning was that she and her friends had all agreed to dress in eighties fashion that day. "I made the shirt myself. It's cute and cool. I understand if you don't get it," she said.

Excuse me! I had told her she could dance her butt back upstairs and try again, or else I would introduce her to another popular fashion trend: mom jeans.

I put two silver dollars on her plate.

"Hold the bacon please, just some eggs." She picked up the glass of orange juice I poured for her, sniffed it, then promptly put it back where she had found it.

"You touched it. You finish it," I said.

After breakfast, Lucy helped Po Po load the dishwasher. Ryan took the trash out to the curb. Me? Well, I delegated.

We said goodbye to Po Po and got out the door on time. I always drove the kids to school before heading into the office.

I sat behind the wheel of my Charger and turned the key in the ignition. The 370-hp Hemi V8 engine rumbled to life and vibrated my butt cheeks. I loved my balls.

After dropping off the kids, I turned onto Polk Street and caught green lights one after another. It wasn't even nine yet, and I was already slaying Monday.

I hit speakerphone on my cell and dialed Agent Tracy House. She worked in the Oakland field office and was also one of my closest friends in the bay.

"So next week is Kyle's one-year anniversary with the Bureau. I thought the three of us, Po Po, and the kids could get together for a celebratory dinner."

Yes, Detective Kyle Kang of the San Francisco Police Department had become a field agent with the FBI. After working the Chasing Chinatown case together, I convinced him to come over to our side. He did twenty weeks at Quantico, and my supervisor, Scott Reilly, talked to the right people and had him based in San Francisco. We were officially partners.

"Sounds great. Has it been a year already?" she asked.

"I know. It seems like only yesterday that I had to school the little whippersnapper on the fine art of law enforcement."

We both laughed.

"I'm sure he would disagree with your assessment," she said.

I pulled my vehicle into the underground parking structure of the Phillip Burton Federal Building and parked. "Hey, listen, I'm about to lose service. We'll talk later."

I took the elevator up to the lobby level so I could pass through security.

"Agent Kane. Good morning."

"Officer Gordon. Same to you," I said as I put my purse on the conveyer belt for the x-ray machine. I handed him my sidearm and my identification. "You have a good weekend?"

"Grilled rib eyes, drank beer, watched football—pre-season has started. It's my happy place until I'm back here. Did you hear about the kid?"

I shook my head.

"Some sick parent stuffed their kid into a suitcase and left her outside the building this morning."

"What? Like a baby?"

"From what I heard she was older, maybe ten. SFPD took her to the hospital to get her looked over."

I cringed. "That's terrible. I think I prefer your steak-and-football story."

I picked up my belongings on the other side of security and then rode the elevator up to the thirteenth floor. Most of the agents arrived around nine. Many were already on calls or tapping away at their laptops. I made a beeline toward the staff kitchen and fixed a cup of my favorite: tieguanyin tea. I always kept a tin of loose leaves on me.

I settled into my desk amongst the others. Even though I had significant seniority—assistant special agent in charge—I didn't have an office. Didn't want one. I liked being out in the open with the rest of the field agents.

I'd always been that way, even when I lived in Hong Kong and served as the chief inspector in charge of Organized Crime and Triad Bureau for HKP. I didn't hide away in a big office. I sat with my team. I'd have it no other way—then or now.

From the corner of my eye, I spotted Kang walking toward me with his lanky strides. He stood over six feet and often appeared a bit awkward to those who didn't know him, but he had quickly become the best partner ever, and friend. He still dressed the same as he did when he was a detective: dark-colored suits purchased off the rack from the local department store. I liked that familiar quality about him.

He was chatting on his cell phone when he sat down at the desk opposite me. He smiled and mouthed, *Sokolov.*

Detective Pete Sokolov had been his partner at SFPD.

When they worked together, they were often referred to as The Wall and The Curtain.

"Yeah, send it to me. We'll see if you got the goods," he said before disconnecting the call.

"What did he get his hands on?" I asked.

"He said he found your doppelganger."

Just then Kang's phone chimed, and he tapped at the screen.

"Holy moly!"

CHAPTER SIX

"It's you! It really is."

"You know the problem with doppelgangers," I said as I stood up and made my way around the desks to his side. "Everyone thinks it's an exact look-alike except the person who is the comparison— Holy crap!"

"You were saying?"

I snatched the phone out of his hand for a closer look. I simply couldn't believe it. I'd had people send me photos before, claiming they'd found my twin, but I never once thought they'd nailed it. In fact, it often made me a bit angry because those "doppelgangers" always looked odd or unpleasant or simply ugly. *Oh my God. Is that what I really look like?* It's enough to mess with your head.

"I don't know what to say... She's like a mini-me."

"Did Sokolov nail it or what?"

Her nose.

That black hair.

Even her eyes were green like mine.

Flashbacks of my childhood popped into my head as I stared

at the phone; it was as if I were seeing myself as a little girl. Granted she still looked like a child; it wasn't as if she looked like an adult version of me, but nobody could miss the connection.

"Cute kid. Is she your daughter?"

Agent Oliver Hansen was looking over my shoulder at the screen. He was freshly minted out of Quantico. While he only had seven months of the job under his belt, he had incredible street smarts and was a quick learner. He also always had freshly minted breath. I had taken a liking to him and often involved him and his partner with the investigations I oversaw.

"She's not my daughter."

"Wait, I thought you had a daughter. I swear I heard you mention it before."

"I do have daughter, but this isn't her."

"My old partner at SFPD sent me this picture," Kang chimed in. "They found her outside our offices." He pointed toward a window. "Child abandonment."

"Oh my God," I said. "One of the FPS officers downstairs mentioned this to me. This must be the girl he was talking about."

"Didn't he see the connection? I mean, it's pretty obvious," Kang said.

I shook my head. "He said the girl had been taken away by the time he arrived."

"You talking about the guy who always grills steaks and watches football on the weekends?"

"Yeah, why?"

Kang shrugged. "Nothing."

"What?" I crinkled my brow.

"Just find it weird that he does the same thing every weekend."

"It's football season. Thousands of people do this every weekend."

"I'm just saying. You know, in general. He could mix it up."

I looked at Hansen. "Is it me or is he not making any sense?"

Hansen shrugged.

"Hold on," Kang said. "How does saying someone does the same thing every weekend not make any sense? Sounds pretty clear to me. Hansen, isn't it pretty clear?"

"Uh, well... I think you're both right."

"Come on. Just pick a side." Kang gave him a friendly wink. "There's no wrong answer here."

"There could be." I doubled down with a toothy grin.

"In that case, I side with Assistant Special Agent in Charge Abby Kane. Sorry, Agent Kang, she outranks you." He called his partner, Agent Patrick Pratt, to come and look at the photograph.

"Whoa. That's definitely your twin," Pratt said to Abby. "Do you have a picture of yourself at that age? It would be neat to see the comparison."

More agents began to huddle around and gawk at the picture. I wasn't sure who had said it first, but eventually we all started to refer to her as Suitcase Girl.

Deep in conversation, not a one of us saw our boss, Special Agent in Charge Scott Reilly, approaching.

"Where's Kane?"

"I'm here." I poked my head out from the huddle.

"You and your partner! My office! Now!"

It's never good when he calls me by my last name.

CHAPTER SEVEN

KANG and I trailed behind Reilly, walking the length of the carpeted corridor sandwiched by cubed offices. I couldn't help but wonder what the hell we had done to merit the attitude. It really wasn't like Reilly to show his temper. *Unless...*

That's what it is. The higher-ups are riding his arse.

We hung a left into his office. In the years I had worked for him, the décor had always remained the same. Except recently he had acquired a potted floor plant, a Pachira or money plant. The metal blinds that shaded the large window behind his desk were always kept angled downward. He liked peering at the street below.

Reilly scooted around the large oak desk and took a seat before removing his glasses and setting them down on a stack of manila folders. Usually his desk was a battlefield of folders and paper. That day everything was arranged into neat piles. *I give it a few hours before it looks like a bomb exploded on his desk.*

Behind him was a credenza. The familiar photo of his daughter sat on top of it in a silver frame. She had gone missing when she was only twenty-two. Cold case.

He rubbed his eyes. "Look, there's no easy way to say this, so I'll just say it. I'm getting heat from the deputy director on the Dead Red Operation."

The Dead Red Operation was a big deal for the FBI. A task force had been put together that involved the CIA, the Department of Homeland Security, the National Security Agency, Border Protection, and Immigration. It was ongoing, and its purpose was to determine and neutralize credible terrorist threats aimed at the US from China.

Most people thought our biggest threat was the Middle East, and it was, but China had become increasingly aggressive over the last few years, moving beyond hacking our government servers. Every agent in the office had a piece of the operation on his or her plate.

It was a necessary pain in the butt.

Why?

The Department of Justice wanted to see operations foiled and cells dismantled. Monitoring chatter wasn't good enough. And anyway, the NSA had a monopoly on that. What they expected from us was actionable intel that led to arrests.

About a month ago, Kang had received a tip that a small accounting firm was moving money from China into the US. If we could identify the players and follow the money, we figured it might lead us to an underground cell, one that hadn't yet caught our attention.

It took us two weeks just to execute a black-bag job, where we survey a business or a home to figure out how to infiltrate and plant RF bugs. Once we had the place tapped, we conducted surveillance from a van near the business. We also utilized a stingray: a tracking device capable of capturing calls made by cell phones. Kang and I would sit inside the vehicle all day, listening to conversations taking place over the phone and on the premise. We had been actively listening for a week and had absolutely nothing to show for it.

"Unless you come up with something substantial today, I'm pulling the plug on the wire."

"But—"

"Abby, we can't keep listening if nothing's coming of it. Not to mention it's a waste of resources. You're one of the best agents I have. No offense, Kang."

"None taken."

"I need you on something that will yield results."

"It's only been a week. I just think we—"

"Don't think. Your time is up unless you deliver me something actionable by end of day."

Reilly put his glasses back on and started tapping on his laptop.

Needless to say, Kang and I were both a bit shocked at the abrupt ending to our little operation. Reilly looked back up at us.

"Last I heard, the federal government wasn't paying you two to sit."

Message received. We left the office.

"What just happened?" Kang asked as we walked back to our desks.

"We got axed. That's what."

"Can he do that?"

"He can and just did."

"For some reason I thought only crap like that happened at the city level. We're FBI, the federal government. We can do whatever we want."

"Ha! Whatever gave you that impression?"

"You," he said, jerking his head back.

"Oh..." I started gathering my stuff from my desk.

"Plus now you're the assistant special agent in charge at the office."

"Big deal."

"Abby, you're second in command here. Soon you'll have Reilly's job and be running this office."

"Nah," I waved him off. "Too much paperwork and politics. Who needs that? I like being in the field."

Hansen walked over from his desk and in a low voice asked, "Hey, boss, what did the big man want? He sounded pissed earlier."

"He's pulling our surveillance detail. If we want to save it, we have the day to produce something, anything," I said.

"That sucks."

"Yeah, a big one."

"Has he mentioned what you might be doing if he does pull it? Pratt and I are dying to get our hands dirty on something you're working on, so if there's an opportunity..." He flashed a smile.

"Don't worry; I'll let you know."

Hansen clucked his tongue. "Good luck." He gave Kang a slap on the arm before walking away.

Once Hansen had walked out of earshot, Kang leaned toward me with a smirk on his face. "Me thinks he has a crush on the bossy boss."

I slipped my purse strap over my shoulders and whispered back, "Maybe. At least he doesn't get jealous like you."

CHAPTER EIGHT

KANG and I continued to battle back and forth over which one of us was more the jealous type as we drove. Since we'd first met, there was always playful flirting in our relationship. We never seriously acted on it, but maybe that was why we got along so well.

Our destination was the accounting offices of Woo & Sons in the Richmond District. This was the city's second Chinatown, a neighborhood where a number of affluent and middle-class Chinese families lived.

Woo & Sons was a small firm—just the owner, Arthur Woo, and four other associates, including his eldest son. The office was on 6th Avenue, just south of Clement Street. We always parked our vehicle on Clement. Out of eyesight but close enough that we could still listen in.

Kang moved the gearshift to neutral and set the parking brake. "Just admit you were insanely jealous over Suzi."

She was Kang's last girlfriend, and I despised her. And yes, I'll admit... at the time, I sort of, maybe, had a crush on Kang. But I also knew, before she came into the picture, he had a crush on me. The problem back then was one of us was always in a relationship. Now that we worked together permanently, it definitely wouldn't happen.

"You see that's where you're wrong," I said. "I wasn't jealous over Sushi—"

"Calling her names... isn't that a sign of jealousy?"

"Pbbbffftttt, I just didn't like her. Plus I wanted to be a good friend for you."

"What, by breaking us up?" A large smile formed on his face.

"Well, yeah, I mean, you were so whipped there was no way you could see the scaly dragon under that pancake foundation she always wore. You—" I pointed at him. "You should be thanking me."

"If we're talking about giving thanks here, then you should be thanking me for saving you from that hippie, Green."

Dr. Timothy Green was the top medical examiner in the city. We often worked cases together.

"Save?" I cocked an eyebrow. "Puullease, Green is practically my height, which ain't much. I didn't need saving, and anyway, he's always been a perfect gentleman. He's nice."

Kang waved my answer off with his hand. "You just like the attention. I'm getting a box from Schubert's. I'll be right back."

With Kang gone, I busied myself with setting up the equipment. I hooked a laptop up to the stingray and then powered up the surveillance device. Cell phones are always searching for the nearest cell tower, even when they aren't making a call. All the stingray does is trick the phone into thinking it's a tower. It then collects the data without the cell phone knowing before passing it on to the actual tower. That allowed us to target specific phones. Easy peasy.

The car door opened, and Kang slipped inside with that familiar cardboard box. "I got two Neapolitans, two cherry tarts, and two slices of opera cake."

"Yes!" I held my hand up, and Kang high-fived me.

He slipped off his jacket and rubbed his hands together before picking up a Neapolitan and taking a large bite. The flakey crust exploded at the corners of his mouth and sprinkled across the front of his shirt.

I grabbed a plastic fork and targeted the opera cake. The hazelnut-flavored sponge cake layered with chocolate and mocha praline was out of this world. If possible, we always kept conversation to a minimum while we stuffed our faces.

Kang adjusted his headset over his ears. He monitored the bug we had inside the office. I tracked the calls made from Arthur's cell phone.

"He's on a call," I said. "It's his girlfriend. She wants to go shopping."

Arthur Woo was mid-fifties, his girlfriend was mid-twenties, and his wife was mid-forties.

I let out a defeated breath. If this call was any indication of how our day was headed, there would be no saving this operation.

I took another bite of cake. "You think maybe we got it all wrong?"

Kang tilted his head from side to side. "My informant has always been reliable. I wouldn't have pushed for all of this," he motioned around us, "if I didn't think there was something here. Why, you thinking otherwise?"

"No, sounded credible and worthwhile. I mean, it had to have been or else we would have never been given the go ahead.

It's just weird that there's nothing. Aside from cheating on his wife, Woo's business seems pretty legit."

"You know, it could be that they aren't discussing anything over the phone or in person."

"I doubt the Chinese are using email. It's a sure paper trail. Plus, Woo is using a burner cell. I don't believe it's because his real cell phone is broken. I just wish we had something that would convince Reilly to let us listen for a bit longer. I'd like to know how often Woo changes phones."

"You think maybe they're on to us?"

I took a moment to think about that. "Eh... if they are, it's probably the name painted on the decoy van that gave us away."

"Aw, come on. Give it up already."

"What?" I shrugged. "I said probably, not definitely."

We were using a commercial painting business as our cover. Kang had fallen in love with the name the Great Wall of Paint, featuring an image of the Great Wall made out of paint cans.

"I distinctly remember telling you that sounded too fake."

"Oh and 'Easy Painting,'" he used his hands to produce an imaginary marquee, "'You point. We paint.' is a better choice?"

"Sounds more legit to me."

The truth was both names sucked, but we'd flipped a coin and Kang won.

"You're just used to having everything your way, and this time the tarot cards dealt a different fate." Kang smiled.

I laughed.

He laughed.

I threw a fake punch at his arm and then quickly followed up with a double punch. "Two for flinching."

CHAPTER NINE

Benito Decker, the FPS officer who had found the suitcase, lived at an address in a nondescript area of the city. The neighborhood was too far south to be considered Lower Fillmore and too far north to be part of Hayes Valley. It wasn't the greatest neighborhood, rough around the edges but affordable in pricey San Francisco.

Sokolov parked the Crown Vic next to a small apartment building at the corner of Laguna and McAllister Streets.

"Little odd for an FPS officer to be living in a neighborhood like this," Bennie remarked. "You think his pay grade would afford him something more."

"Maybe he likes to spend his money on something other than rent," Sokolov said, exiting the vehicle.

The building stood three-stories high and had a neutral color. Four large garage doors occupied the ground floor. Facing the street on the second and third floor were bay windows. A single door led inside the building, revealing a small foyer where there was a staircase with a dark wood banister. No elevator.

Sokolov led the way to the second floor and stopped next to

a door identified by a tarnished-brass number one. He knocked three times, shaking the door in the process.

"Mr. Decker," Sokolov called out. "This is SFPD. Would you mind opening up? We'd like to ask you a few questions."

The door cracked open, and a young man with a buzz haircut, who looked like he needed sleep, poked his head out. He wore an undershirt and blue shorts.

"Hey, come inside. My CO called me earlier and said someone might be stopping by." He stepped aside, allowing them to enter.

"We're sorry to disturb you." Sokolov turned his body sideways as he walked through the doorway. "We'll try to make this as quick as possible."

"You guys want coffee? I brewed a pot not too long ago."

"We're fine."

"The place is a little small," he said. "Not much room to maneuver."

The one-bedroom apartment had a small sitting area and a kitchen. The mismatched furniture probably came with the place.

"As soon as the lease is up, I'm moving into a bigger apartment. I was in a pinch and needed a place quick."

"You not from around here?" Bennie asked.

"No sir. I'm fresh out of training in Glynco, Georgia. This is actually my first position—night shift." He smiled. "Take a seat?"

"We're fine standing," Sokolov said. "Why don't you tell us in your own words what happened this morning."

"Well, I was sitting at my post, the information counter. It was time for my next round. It was quiet. No problems at all."

"Do these rounds take you outside the building?"

"No, we don't patrol outside, but I do walk to the entrance for a visibility check. Like I said earlier, everything was fine. So I returned to my post. A little later I went to the bathroom. I wasn't gone longer than ten minutes."

"How do you know that?" Bennie asked.

He chuckled. "We have to log the time we leave and return. So that's how I know."

"And when you came back, that's when you noticed the suitcase?"

"No, it wasn't until I did my next round about an hour later. The electronic security machine at the entrance blocks almost all visibility outside from where I sit. That's why we're required to walk up to the door during our rounds. So anyway, that's when I spotted the suitcase. A bomb was the first thing that crossed my mind. I was about to call my CO when the suitcase literally moved, like it tilted from side to side. I moved a little closer, and it did it again. That's when I decided to go outside and check."

"How did you know it wasn't a bomb?" Bennie asked. "You could have gotten yourself blown up."

"Because the second time, the suitcase moved like someone or something was inside of it. I guess I broke protocol there, but I called my CO shortly after."

"And that's when you discovered the little girl."

He nodded. "Yeah, of course. She was shivering. I put my jacket over her and brought her inside right away. My CO told me to call SFPD. I did. They showed up about thirty minutes later."

"The girl... she say anything while she was in your custody?"

"Not a word. I tried to get her to tell me how she ended up

in the suitcase, but she never answered. I know some guy left her because I reviewed the video footage, but she never said anything about him. I'm sorry, but I didn't push questioning her because I was told it was an SFPD matter, which I found strange since technically the area outside the building is federal property, or at least it's space leased by the federal government. Anyway, how is the girl? Is she okay?"

"She's fine. We just came from the hospital. No signs of physical abuse. Most likely a case of child abandonment."

"That's a shame." Decker folded his arms across his chest. "Seems like a nice kid. I can't believe a parent would do such a thing."

"You'd be surprised what some parents will do to their kids."

CHAPTER TEN

Sokolov and Bennie thanked Decker and made their way down the staircase and out of the building.

"Everything he said corroborates what his supervisor told us and what we saw on the tape," Bennie said before sitting inside the vehicle. "I got no reason not to believe him. What are you thinking?"

"I agree but—"

"The suitcase."

Sokolov grunted. "If this was treated as a case of child abandonment from the beginning, then no evidence was collected from the scene."

"Well, there's the suitcase. They should have bagged it. Outside of that, there's the rape kit, but from what I understand, the backlog at the crime lab is hell."

"It's better now. Before, it took about nine months to generate a DNA profile. Now it's three months."

"Damn, that's still a long time."

"The whole place went through the wringer a few years ago

when it was discovered that the lab mishandled DNA
evidence."

"What? Like overturn-the-case type of mishandling?"

"Yeah. Over one thousand cases were audited."

"At least they're fixing it."

"There are a lot of things that need fixing in this city."

Bennie shifted in his seat. "Listen, when we get back to the
precinct, I'll check and see if the suitcase was dusted for prints.
If anything, it'll help missing persons."

"I think we should have CSI cover the scene."

"Probably contaminated by now."

"Probably, but the suitcase... Something doesn't feel right."
Sokolov licked his lips.

"I think it's our natural reaction. Suitcase equals foul play."

"Maybe you're right."

Bennie slapped his thighs. "Bottom line is the girl's not
dead, and it doesn't seem like she's been hurt. At the most this is
a case of abandonment. This is a missing persons/CPS problem.
We're Homicide."

Sokolov stared straight ahead at the road with one hand
resting on top of the steering wheel. "When you have the tech
check the suitcase for prints, have him swing by the hospital and
print the girl."

"Will do. You know if the captain finds out what we're
doing, he ain't going to be too happy about it."

"Right now he thinks we're working a homicide," Sokolov
said.

"Yeah, but sending us was a screw-up. I'd be surprised if this
girl is still listed on the board when we get back. I bet the case
has already been transferred to missing persons."

"They're overworked and understaffed. Trust me, if it has, they don't even know about it yet."

"Okay, so if it becomes a problem, we'll just say we were helping out... tying up loose ends."

"It'll buy us a day. Maybe we can help this kid. If her parents don't show up, she'll end up in the system and her life will be screwed."

CHAPTER ELEVEN

WE WERE NEARING four in the afternoon, the cut-off time that Reilly had given us. If we hadn't anything to support our allegations by then, we were to pack up and call it a day.

And we had zip.

Nada.

Zilch.

Our month-long operation was a complete bust.

And it pissed me off.

I always prided myself on being productive and solving cases—I put the bad guys behind bars. The Woo operation would now be a black eye on my resume. Ugh.

"Come on now. It's not the end of the world," Kang said as he shut down the scanner. "This is part of the job. It happens. Imagine if we hadn't chased it and it turned out to be something."

He was right, but still I hated the feeling it left in my stomach. "Hey, you still have that picture of Suitcase Girl?"

"Hang on," he said.

I crawled toward the front of the van and eased myself into

the passenger seat. Kang placed his butt in the driver seat and then forwarded the picture to me.

"It's a little freaky how much she looks like me," I said, staring at the photo.

Kang started the van, and we drove away.

"Do you know what happens to her now?" I asked.

"If it's a case of child abandonment, she'll be turned over to missing persons. They'll enter her in the system with all the other missing children. I imagine CPS is already involved."

"It's a shame. She looks so sweet. Why would her parents ditch her like that? Such a cruel thing to do."

"There are a lot of messed-up folks in this world. You seem to have taken an interest in the girl."

"I guess it's because I look at her and see a part of me. Makes me wonder if I'd had a daughter of my own... would she look like her?"

I continued to look at the photo of Suitcase Girl. Kang continued to drive. Neither of us spoke.

We probably would have stayed that way until we reached the office, but Kang dialed a number on his cell phone. He switched it to speakerphone, and I heard the ringing.

"Sokolov," the voice said on the other end.

"It's Kang and Kane here."

"How's life in the van? I'm sure those are the type of investigations that made jumping ship to the FBI all worth it. Oh the jealousy," he said dryly before chuckling.

"Yeah, yeah, keep it up," I said. "And I'll figure out a way to include you on a joint task force that takes place in this van."

"What's up?" Sokolov asked.

"The Suitcase Girl," Kang said, "Where are you guys on the case?"

"Nowhere really because technically it's not our case. We're doing a little follow-up, but it'll be turned over to missing persons. The girl is at Saint Francis. The doctor said she checked out okay. No signs of physical or sexual abuse but they did a rape kit anyway. CPS is already involved. They'll be back tomorrow morning to take custody of the girl."

"Any idea how she ended up in the suitcase?" I asked.

"There's video footage. Shows a lone man dropping off the suitcase in the early morning. We spoke with the FPS officer on watch. He just happened to be on a bathroom break when it happened. He didn't see the suitcase until an hour later on his next round."

"Did the man look related?"

"Too dark to tell. We tried talking to the girl, but she's tightlipped. Hasn't said a single word to anyone since FPS found her."

"She's probably in shock," Kang said.

"What's with the interest?" Sokolov asked. "You guys getting involved? We're having a guy print her. It would be helpful if you could run it through your database."

"Sure, no problem," I said. "Were you able to determine her age?"

"The doctor thinks she's between ten and twelve."

"You seem to know a lot about her situation for someone who should be investigating homicides," I said.

"It's the suitcase. Why stuff the girl inside and leave her there?"

"Yeah, seems like extra effort for abandonment," Kang said.

"Unless... the intent wasn't abandonment," Sokolov responded.

"You think a dead girl should have been found instead?" I asked.

"The lab at the hospital found traces of a sedative in her blood, enough to put her out. I wondered if it was intended to do more."

"Interesting premise," Kang said.

"If I discover anything else, we'll let you guys know," Sokolov said.

Kang disconnected the call. "We can run the girl's prints, see if we get a hit, but you know, not much more."

"This hunch that Sokolov has, it's interesting. Was she supposed to be found dead?"

"I sense the wheels turning in your head. What are you thinking, Abby?"

"The FBI can be involved with missing children if the child is of a tender age, usually twelve and under."

"That's if it's a kidnapping, right? I'm not so sure the evidence is leaning toward that. Sokolov would have pointed that out. This is more along the lines of neglect, poor parenting, that kind of thing."

I shrugged. "Maybe, but like he said, why leave her in a suitcase? Surely it wasn't for easy transport."

"I wouldn't write that thought off so quickly. It seems very probable that it made abandoning the kid easier."

"Saint Francis is near the office. Let's make a quick stop and talk to the girl for a bit."

"Are you serious?"

"Look, I agree—everything we've heard so far points to the girl being abandoned. But I'm with Sokolov. That suitcase creates a ruffle that can't be easily smoothed. I also don't buy that it was used to make abandoning the girl an easier task."

CHAPTER TWELVE

WE ENTERED the hospital's emergency room fifteen minutes later and inquired at the front desk about Suitcase Girl. The nurse sitting behind the counter looked up to find Kang and me showing our identification.

She crinkled her brow. "Are you the mother?"

"No," I said, waving my ID a bit. "We have questions we'd like to ask her. Is that a problem?"

"I'm sorry," she said, a bit flustered. "It's just that you and the little one look alike."

The nurse tapped away at her keyboard while looking at the computer monitor. "She's already been moved to the pediatrics floor, room four."

We took the elevator up two floors and exited, bumping into a family with a child in a wheelchair. Another family sat in the waiting area, their little boy busy playing with a wooden car on an area rug in front of them. The white walls were painted with bright rainbows, colorful flowers, and the characters from the Winnie the Pooh stories.

We walked past the reception desk, straight toward room four. A nurse exited the room just as we approached.

"Oh, you're here. That's good news. Your daughter is fine, a little quiet, but fine."

I held up my identification. "I'm Agent Kane. This is Agent Kang. SFPD brought a young girl in this morning."

"Oh, yes, she's here. I'm sorry. I thought you two were the parents." Her face turned a shade of red before she excused herself.

We watched the nurse hurry away.

"Are you ready to face your twin?" Kang asked with a smile.

"As ready as I'll ever be."

Inside the room, a single gray curtain separated two beds. In the first bed lay a small black girl. A woman sat in a chair next to the bed and held her hand, speaking to her quietly. I smiled at the two as I walked by. The lady smiled back.

I assumed the girl we wanted was on the other side of the curtain. A tingle erupted in my chest and spread outward across my body. I had no idea why it happened. I had questioned hundreds of people of all ages, sexes, and races. Why would this time be any different? *Uh, it's because she looks exactly like you.*

I swallowed right before I turned the corner of the curtain, and then I choked on the quick breath I took.

I stared.

I couldn't help it.

Her eyes, her lips, her nose, her hair—it was like she was modeled after me. Not an exact duplicate. It wasn't like looking in the mirror. Her features were still that of a little girl. Her nose had a more button-like quality, her cheeks were chubbier, her face slightly rounder, but it was clear as day that the similarities were there. Anyone who saw her and then saw me would immediately think she was my daughter. We really did look alike.

Kang cleared his throat, jolting me out of the dream-like state I had suddenly fallen into. I glanced over at him. He had that same dumbstruck look on his face that I imagined was on mine.

I turned my attention back to the girl and said, "Hello. I'm Agent Abby Kane. This is Agent Kyle Kang. We work for the FBI. Is it okay if we talk with you?"

She lay in the bed, sitting upright with her back against two pillows. Her head was turned slightly down, but her eyes were clearly focused on us. A pink blanket covered her from the belly down, and her hands were tucked underneath.

I took a seat in a chair next to the bed. "You must be scared being all alone here. But I don't want you to worry. The nurses here are very good, and they will take care of you."

Not a word from her. She gave no indication through her eyes or any movement that she understood what we were saying.

"Can you tell me your name?"

Empty stare.

"What about the name of your mom and dad, can you tell me that?" I reached out and took hold of her hand, holding it gently. "Can you tell me where you live or go to school?"

The silence from her continued. I looked up at Kang, and he offered a shrug. I stood up. As I turned to walk away, the girl grabbed my arm, stopping me.

I sat back down in the chair, her eyes locked on mine the entire time.

"So you understand what I'm saying? Nod if I'm right."

A beat later she nodded.

I let out a breath of relief. *Progress.*

"She understands English so language isn't an issue," Kang said.

"How old are you?" I held up ten fingers. "Ten?"

She shook her head no.

I held up one finger. "Eleven?"

She shook her head no.

"Twelve?"

She nodded yes.

"What about your name, sweetie. Do you remember what it is?"

This time she didn't acknowledge me, and her gaze fell to her lap.

"Do you live in San Francisco?" I asked.

This time she shook her head no. *Okay, this is good.*

"Can you tell me where?"

"You probably need to ask her the question in a way she can answer with a head nod," Kang suggested.

"Do you live in Oakland?"

No response.

I continued my line of questioning, naming the major surrounding cities, but none of them elicited a response from her. To be honest, there were hundreds of cities I could rattle off.

She yawned, and her eyes closed slightly. I removed one of my business cards from my purse and placed it in her hand. "If you want to talk or if you remember anything, just tell a nurse and they will call me. Okay?"

She gripped the card, shut her eyes, and a few seconds later, fell asleep.

Once we were out of the room, I turned to Kang as we

walked back to the elevator. "There's a chance she's not from this state. Interstate comes under federal jurisdiction."

"It does, but crossing state lines to abandon a child is still abandonment. I think we need a stronger case to convince Reilly," he said.

"I think the suitcase is our trump card. It's the one thing that makes no sense. Add in the sedative and the thinking that maybe she wasn't supposed to be found alive, and we might have enough cause to spend some time digging."

CHAPTER THIRTEEN

The aroma hit me the moment I walked through the front door: aniseed, chili, garlic, ginger, and Chinese cinnamon. Combined with the hissing of the wok I heard coming from the kitchen, I knew a Sichuan treat awaited me. My favorite style of cooking followed by Hunan. Po Po was well versed in both styles.

"Mmmm, something smells good," I called out as I closed the front door to our Victorian home.

From the entrance I had nearly a straight view down the narrow hallway that ran the length of the house. The kitchen was at the midway point, and I headed straight toward it.

Lucy stuck her head out from the kitchen doorway. "Mommy, you're home," she said. "I'm helping Po Po with dinner."

"Look at you. Soon you'll be the second best cook in the house." I gave Lucy a kiss on her forehead.

I entered the open kitchen. Po Po had just finished scooping the last of a dish from the wok and into a serving bowl. I looked over her shoulder and spied Mapo tofu. One of my favorite dishes. "Smells wonderful." I gave her a peck on the cheek.

"Lucy, where's your brother?"

"He's upstairs taking a shower." She took the serving dish from Po Po and headed toward the dining room.

"Anything I can help with?" I asked.

"No," Po Po replied. "Everything finish already."

As usual, Po Po wore one of the three different housedresses she owned, at least that was what it seemed like to me. That night she wore the light-blue one with tiny white flowers, white terry cloth slippers on her feet. They made a swish-swish sound on the wooden floors.

She handed me a pot filled with rice. "Go, go," she said as she pushed me out of the kitchen.

The dining room table had already been set. "I did this all by myself," Lucy said with a smile.

"That's very nice of you to help Po Po. Did your brother help?"

"What do you think?" Lucy rested her hands on her hips and did her best to cock an eyebrow. It really only looked like she was opening one eye wider.

Po Po shuffled to the dining room table carrying a pot of green tea. She placed it down and then told Lucy to call her brother. The child walked to the bottom of the steps and then proceeded to yell her brother's name.

"Lucy!" I said. "Go upstairs and get him. Don't yell."

I turned back to the table and eyed the dishes. "This looks wonderful. Let me guess. I know this is Mapo tofu. That's Sichuan dry-fried green beans. That's Kung Pao chicken, one of Ryan's favorites. This is…" I peered closer. "Stuffed eggplant fried in garlic?"

Po Po nodded.

"That's one you love. And this last dish I already know Lucy loves: Dandan noodles."

In fact, the entire family loved that dish. Dandan noodles were nothing more than simple street food. A small bowl of wheat noodles served with a topping of your choosing. Po Po always prepared a stir-fried mixture of ground pork, chili, garlic, ginger, vinegar, and a selection of spices she wouldn't divulge.

There was a time when I felt extremely threatened by my mother-in-law's ability to keep a home. My domestic skills paled in comparison to hers. She watched everything I did, closely. It made me feel as if I would never live up to her standards, especially when my late husband, Peng, her son, was still alive. It was hard back then.

Nowadays, I didn't get worked up over it. I'd accepted that I would never be as good as she. So rather than feel inferior at the dinner table, I opted for feeling hungry and simply enjoying the gift that is her cooking.

The kids entered the dining room.

"Hi, Abby," Ryan said as he pulled a chair out and sat.

"Aren't you forgetting something?"

He got up, walked over to me, and gave me a hug and a kiss.

We have a tradition at our house during meals—mostly it's observed during dinner. For the first ten minutes or so, we focus on eating. There was no murmur of conversation, only the sounds of slurping and chopsticks tinkling against bowls. I mean, one could try to ask a question, but no one would answer. That was just the way it was in our family.

Sit.

Eat.

Talk.

That was the preferred order. Once we had quelled our hunger to some degree, we'd open our mouths to communicate.

"Ryan, you showered late today," I said.

He swallowed a mouthful. "Yeah, I stayed later at the dojo helping another student. It's all good though. I like helping out."

"Lucy, how was your day? Anything exciting happen in school?"

"You mean besides me not wearing the best possible eighties outfit ever?"

"Wasn't that last week?"

"It was, but my friends still bring it up because I was the only one who didn't participate."

"Awww," I said as I pretended to wipe tears from my eyes. "Besides that."

"It was a normal day." She slurped on some noodles.

"Oh, I almost forgot," I said. "Guess what happened to me today? I discovered I have a doppelganger."

"Doppel-what?" Lucy asked, again trying to cock her eyebrow but failing.

I pulled up the photo of Suitcase Girl on my phone and then showed it to everyone.

"Wow, she looks just like you," Ryan said, grabbing hold of my phone for a closer look.

"Lemme see, lemme see." Lucy hopped off her chair and ran around to the other side of the table where Ryan sat. Po Po sat next to him and leaned over for a better look.

"What do you think, Po Po?" I asked.

She looked up at me and then back at the picture. "Poor thing."

"Holy cow!" Lucy shouted. "She looks like a double of you."

"I know. Weird, huh?"

"Who is she?" Ryan asked.

"We don't know. One of the FPS guards found her abandoned outside our offices."

"Her mom and dad threw her away?" Lucy asked.

"Well, I'm not sure yet. We're trying to figure it out."

Po Po tsked, picked up her chopsticks, and resumed eating.

"I hope you find her mom and dad," Ryan said as he handed my phone back to me. "Is that against the law, to do something like that?"

"It is, if the intent is to cause harm to the child. It's a bit different if she were lost by accident."

"Oh, like the time you lost Lucy in Macy's department store."

"Oh, yeah. I remember when you lost me last Christmas." Lucy smiled at me from her seat.

"I didn't lose you. Stop saying that."

"You lose Lucy?" Po Po asked.

"No, it wasn't anything like that." I waved off the accusation.

"You had the store call her name on the speaker," Ryan continued.

I laughed playfully at his comment. "I was just being thorough."

"I dunno. You looked panicked."

"That's my game face," I mumbled.

"Huh?"

"Look, enough about that. We're talking about this girl and what her parents did. Okay? We have video footage of a man leaving her there, so it wasn't an accident." I left out the suitcase. They didn't need to know that horrible detail.

Ryan picked up his rice bowl. "If her dad left her there, why would you give her back to him?" He shoveled the last of his rice into his mouth with his chopsticks.

"That's a good question. If and when we find her parents, we'll have to determine if she's safe to be back with them."

―――――――

Later that night at the hospital, the night staff had settled into their shifts, visitors were long gone, and all of the patients were asleep. In room four, the lights were off, and the girl in the first bed slept soundly.

But not Suitcase Girl.

Soft grunts escaped her lips while she slept. She kicked her legs before finally turning to her side. Her eyes were jittery under the cover of her lids.

She's walking down a white-walled hallway. Single fluorescent lights run perpendicular above her. A man passes by. He's wearing a long, white coat. He has black hair. She can't see his face. He grabs her hand.

"Hurry," she hears him say as he jerks her arm, prompting her to speed up. "I know you're tired, but it's important we don't stop."

Two other men dressed similarly walk toward them. They're speaking in hushed tones as they pass by.

The man holding her hand stops in front of a stainless steel door. He opens it and orders her to enter the room. She hesitates.

"Come on," the man says, prompting her forward. "Everything will be okay."

He motions for her to enter the room.

Suitcase Girl's eyes shot open, and she gasped. She drew in deep breaths as she tried to recall exactly where she was. Slowly she remembered, and her breathing calmed. She looked at the bedside tray table and grabbed something off of it before sliding her legs over the edge of the bed.

The tile floor was cold against her bare feet and prompted goose pimples to appear on her arms. She walked quietly toward the door, stopping briefly to look at the girl who shared the room with her.

Slowly she turned the door handle and opened the door just a crack. The lights in the hall were off except for one near the nurse's station. A lone nurse sat in a chair behind the counter.

She waited.

She watched.

The nurse stood and walked away from her post, disappearing behind double doors at the end of the hall. Suitcase Girl entered the hallway and hurried toward the station. Picking up the phone, she dialed a number.

For a brief moment I thought I was dreaming, but I wasn't. My phone was ringing. I plopped a hand down on my bedside table and searched until I felt it. I looked at the time. A little after two a.m. *I hope it's not work.*

"This is Kane," I said softly.

No one answered, but I detected ambient noises, maybe breathing. The line was definitely open.

"Hello?" I tried once more. "Can I help you?"

Dead silence. Then the line disconnected.

CHAPTER FOURTEEN

Sokolov sat at his desk. Paperwork covered most of it, though he had cleared a small circle, revealing a table calendar from a few years ago. Drips of coffee stained it. He tore open a white paper bag and removed an overly stuffed chorizo breakfast burrito from inside before flattening the bag into a makeshift plate.

Bennie's desk sat facing flush with Sokolov's, whose desktop was the complete opposite: a laptop, a penholder, a single legal pad, and acres of uncluttered real estate. Bennie had a large coffee with milk and sitting on his makeshift paper-bag plate were three different types of Mexican sweet bread: a concha, a chilindrina, and a chorreada.

He rubbed his hands together. "If I can't have a capuchino cake with my coffee, these three will satisfy."

"This is good," Sokolov said through a mouthful.

"I discovered this place over the weekend," Bennie said as he took a bite of the chorreada and then sipped his coffee.

About two minutes into their breakfast, a booming voice interrupted them.

"Sokolov! Bennie!"

A short, pudgy man wearing an ill-fitted brown suit walked toward them. It was only nine in the morning and already Captain Richard Cavanaugh's forehead bubbled with sweat.

"Why is Jane Doe up there?" he said, pointing at a whiteboard that kept track of the department's outstanding homicides.

"It's a mistake. We know," Sokolov answered. "We're just tying up a few loose ends. There was a suitcase, and we—"

"Whoa, whoa, whoa. Is she dead?"

Sokolov glanced at Bennie before looking Cavanaugh in the eyes. "No, she's not."

"And what does this department investigate?"

Sokolov said nothing.

"Bennie, perhaps you can help your partner with the answer."

Bennie swallowed his bite of food and said, "We investigate homicides."

"That's right. So being that she ain't dead, there can't be a homicide to investigate. Take her name off the board. She's CPS's problem. Am I clear?"

"As always," Sokolov answered with a dismissive breath.

Cavanaugh leaned in and said in a lowered voice, "I don't give a rat's ass if you have a ninety-percent clearance rate, you keep trying me and I'll have your badge."

The captain eyed Bennie before turning around walking back to his office.

Sokolov kept his head down, his right hand squeezed tightly into a ball.

Bennie leaned forward over his desk. "You forgot to tell me

the Cap was a prick." He flashed a smile. "Forget about it. What we did was right. I know his type. He just needs to puff out his chest every now and then to make up for his short, unattractive stature."

Sokolov nodded his head and picked up his burrito. "He's not a prick, and I'm his favorite person." He smiled before taking a bite.

"Well, the girl's been fingerprinted, so has the suitcase, which I found logged in the evidence room. A couple of techs swept the site this morning. I don't know if they found anything. We can forward all of this over to missing persons. At least this stuff will be in a file."

Sokolov chewed and shook his head. "I still think this suitcase is being misread."

"I hear you, but the captain was pretty clear where our efforts need to be focused. I understand you two have the history, but I'm still a newbie... You understand where I'm coming from?"

"I understand. You want to earn his wrath on your own merit." Sokolov chuckled. "Give it another month."

"That quickly, huh?"

"Faster if you're lucky."

———

Kang and I were sitting at our desks. I was munching on a salted bagel with smoked salmon, red onions, and cream cheese. He ate the same thing except his bagel was onion.

"What are the odds Reilly assigns us to a low-profile operation?" he asked.

I swallowed my bite. "Eh, Reilly's not the type to punish like that. He understands one has to investigate in order to determine if there's anything there. Our best bet would be to suggest something to him. It'll give us a little more control over our fate."

"That sounds like a better plan than sitting here and taking what's dished out. You have any thoughts on the ongoing investigations we might jump on?"

"I do. There's one that has absolutely no attention by anyone in the office."

"Tell me you're not talking about Suitcase Girl."

"I am. We established last night that she might not be from this state."

"Barely."

"Doesn't matter; the possibility exists. At a minimum, SFPD will need our help."

"That's if they still have the case."

"Call Sokolov and see if anything new has transpired since our last conversation."

"Sokolov speaking," he said gruffly.

"I would say it sounds like your day is off to a great start, but I know that's how you answer every call."

"I've had better mornings. Cavanaugh's angry about his height again."

"Were you standing next to him and looking down?"

"Nah, I sat while I looked down at him."

"Good one. Listen, I'm calling about Suitcase Girl. Where are you guys with the case?"

"Nowhere. That's the beef I had with Cavanaugh. We can't touch it."

"I see."

"Why?"

"Last night when we spoke to the girl, we got the impression she might be from another state. That could make it a federal case. We were thinking joint task force."

"Another task force with the FBI? Yeah, that's exactly what Cavanaugh is looking for. You'll have to find a way to force his hand, but if you guys do move ahead, we can forward everything we have."

"All right. I'll let you know where we land."

Kang disconnected the call. "Remember my old captain, Cavanaugh?"

"Yeah..."

"He pulled the case from them. It's dead there."

"What about a task force?"

"You know Cavanaugh's not a fan of working with you or the FBI."

"I know. That's why I try to make it happen as often as possible."

"Also, it didn't sound like they made any progress with the case. If we take it on, they'll send over the file. Who were you talking to?"

With Kang busy speaking to Sokolov, I had called the hospital to see if Suitcase Girl was still there. She wasn't. CPS had already collected her, but they gave me the name and number of the caseworker.

"Christine Rosales is the caseworker assigned to Suitcase Girl. She's already taken possession of the girl and transferred her to a women's shelter. I thought we could question the girl again, see if we can make more progress before pitching Reilly."

Kang glanced at his wristwatch. "We better hurry out of here before he calls us into his office."

CHAPTER FIFTEEN

ROSALES WAS at the local women's shelter talking to Miranda Massey, the shelter's director of mental health, when her cell phone rang. She had a brief conversation and then slid the phone back into her purse.

"You'll never guess who that was," she said.

Massey shrugged. "Who?"

"The FBI. Apparently they have an interest in the girl I just brought here."

"Really? Well, that has to be a good thing. Someone's investigating."

"It should. The agent I spoke to didn't go into details, only that they wanted to question the girl again."

"They've already spoken to her once?"

"Apparently they stopped by the hospital after I left. I wasn't aware of it. I'll stay and supervise the next conversation."

"You're always welcome here," Massey said.

"You were saying before the call, about the girl..."

"Oh yes, about the girl. It's completely normal for a child to clam up after a traumatic experience. Often a big part of their refusal to speak is because they simply can't remember. The memory loss is temporary and usually only lasts for a few days, a week in more extreme cases. It all depends on the experience the child was put through."

"How would you rank being locked inside a suitcase and left outside in the cold?"

"It's not the worst that I've seen, but it's up there. It really depends on the child. Some handle situations better than others. If you don't mind, I'd like to have a few words with her alone before the FBI arrives."

"I'll be right here if you need me," Rosales said.

Kang drove. He had traded in his beloved Crown Vic for one of the agency-issued SUVs shortly after joining the Bureau and never regretted it.

"I don't know why you don't requisition one of these vehicles," he said. "It's great."

"Meh, I like my sporty beast."

We arrived at the shelter not long after I'd ended my call with Rosales. It was housed inside a funky, bay-window-laden building located in the Mission on 18th Street. Colorful murals depicting women of all races, ages, and sizes involved in various activities like farming, cooking, teaching, and so forth covered most of the building.

The entrance led to a large, open space with a few couches and sitting chairs. A young woman sat behind a small desk. Murals, in the same style as the ones on the outside of the building, graced the walls inside.

I spied an old upright piano with a red-velvet padded

bench. Whenever I see a piano, I regret not paying more attention during the lessons my father paid for when I was a child. As it stands, if the playlist calls for a loop of *Heart and Soul*, then I'm your gal.

Kang and I must have stuck out like a sore thumb in our suits because before we made it to the reception desk a woman approached us.

"Are you Agent...?" She trailed off, her expression one of surprise—eyes wide, mouth hanging open.

I produced my identification. "I'm Agent Kane, and this is Agent Kang."

The woman still hadn't closed her mouth.

"Is there something wrong?" I asked.

"I'm sorry." She shook her head and blinked excessively. "It's just that... Has anyone told you—"

"The girl and I look alike. Yes, I'm aware of it."

"The resemblance is incredible. I'm sorry." She held out her hand. "I'm Christine Rosales, Child Protection Services."

Everyone shook hands.

"I understand that both of you had a chance to talk to the girl yesterday at the hospital.

"We did. Just a few questions."

"As her caseworker, I have to say this. You're not allowed to question her alone. I need to be there."

"Protocol. Gotcha," I said.

"I'm glad you understand. So am I to assume the FBI's interest is because you learned something from your first conversation?"

"I wouldn't call it a breakthrough, but we heard enough to believe she may not be from California."

"Oh?"

"She didn't actually answer our questions like you would expect. She either nodded 'yes' or shook her head 'no' when asked closed-ended questions. We determined that she's twelve. I rattled off most of the major surrounding cities, and she indicated 'no' to them all."

"Interesting leap. Regardless of the reason, I'm glad you're involved."

"Where is she?" I asked.

"She's being settled in by Miranda Massey; she's in charge of the center. When I spoke with her earlier, she said it's normal for a child who's gone through a traumatic experience such as this to experience temporary memory loss. If her recovery goes well, she should start to remember."

"We'd love to speak with her now, seeing as we made some progress yesterday."

Just then a woman in her fifties wearing a light-colored, paisley skirt with a white blouse appeared. She had long, brown hair streaked with white and kept it pulled back into a braided ponytail that hung just past the middle of her back. Her face was makeup-free but carried a kind smile.

"Welcome. My name is Miranda Massey," she said in a calming voice. "I'm the director here." She clasped her hands and bowed slightly.

"I'm Agent Kane. This is my partner Agent Kang."

"My, my, my. You look exactly like our new guest."

"Yes, she's my doppelganger, or I'm hers, depending on how you want to look at it."

"Agent Kane just finished informing me that she made headway with the girl yesterday via head gestures," Rosales said.

Massey's eyebrows shot upward. "Now that's a positive

thing to hear. The healing has begun. I imagine you want to speak with her now."

"Yes, if that's okay."

"Sure. Follow me."

She led us through a doorway and down a hall. A wooden floorboard squeaked beneath my step. We passed a room where a few young women were watching TV.

"She's staying in a room with four other children, but I'll pull her out so you can conduct your questioning in my office, away from the other residents." Massey pointed at a door. "That's my office. Make yourselves comfortable."

Kang, Rosales, and I waited in her office.

"How long will the shelter care for her?" I asked.

"Usually it's a week to two weeks. Enough time for us to find a placement in a foster home or the parents show up and claim her. Is SFPD still involved?"

"I'm afraid not. They're not recommending criminal charges be filed. As far as they're concerned, she's the responsibility of CPS."

"Figures. Easier to dish her off to us."

"If the parents show up, what are the odds the state will release her into their custody?"

"Depends. I'll interview them and make a visit to the home. The courts will receive my write-up. Really it's up to the judge."

Just then, Massey appeared with Suitcase Girl. She kept her head tilted down as she walked, and her hair fell forward, covering most of her face.

"Hello," I said.

She must have remembered my voice because she looked up immediately and smiled.

"Now that's the first smile I've seen on her face," Rosales said.

I held out my hand. She grabbed hold of it, and I led her over to a chair, where she sat. I bent down so we were looking at each other eye to eye.

"Do you remember me?"

She nodded. It was subtle but clear she was communicating.

"Can you tell me your name?"

Her smile disappeared, and she looked away, shaking her head.

"You don't remember your name?"

She looked at me and then back at the floor.

"It's okay." I gently rubbed her arm. "It may take a few days for you to remember. Do you remember where you live?"

She shook her head no.

"What about the name of your mom and dad, can you tell me that?"

A frown grew on her face.

"It's okay, sweetie, if you can't remember. It's perfectly all right."

I looked up at Massey.

"There's a connection between the two of you," she said. "That's a positive, but she probably needs more time. Usually in cases like this, if family members are involved, we ask them to visit often, to spend time with the child."

"So spending more time with me would help her remember faster?"

"Yes, it would actually."

I turned to Rosales. "Is it possible for me to house her for a couple days, to see if it works? I have the room. I have two children, ages eleven and eight."

"Oh, well, hmmm, you're not the first law enforcement person to make that request. I would have to visit your home." She turned to Massey. "Any objections to Agent Kane housing her?"

"Absolutely not. I think it's a wonderful idea." She looked me straight in the eyes. "Your intentions seem very genuine to me. This can only help the child."

"How soon can I take her?" I asked Rosales.

"Paperwork doesn't take that long to draft. I could drop her off later this evening and inspect the home at the same time."

"Perfect."

CHAPTER SIXTEEN

KANG WAITED until we were out on the sidewalk to ask his question. "You sure you want to house the girl?"

"Why not? If it helps open her up, it'll help with the investigation."

We hopped back inside the SUV and drove off.

"I think it's great what you're doing, but we have yet to officially take over. We need to get Reilly on board, preferably before this investigation escalates."

I dialed Reilly and then switched to speakerphone.

"Reilly speaking"

"It's Kane and Kang. We've got a lead on a missing-persons case from SFPD, a little girl, age twelve. We've already established that she was most likely brought over state lines, so it could be a case of abduction. We'd like two days to investigate our hunch."

"How did you guys get a handle on this?"

"The girl was actually left abandoned outside our offices early yesterday morning. One of the FPS officers found her stuffed inside a suitcase."

"What's SFPD's position on this?"

"Neglect/abandonment. They're not moving ahead with criminal charges. CPS is already involved. We're on our way to Central Station now to talk to the detectives involved."

"Two days, not a minute longer."

The line went dead.

"That was easy," Kang said.

"I told you Reilly was a fair man. We made a case, and it's only two days."

"Let's hope housing her works in our favor," he said.

"It's got to be better than staying at a shelter. Plus, she'll eat well. You know Po Po; she never turns down an opportunity to show off her culinary skills."

"She's a magician in the kitchen. Speaking of food."

Kang made a hard left off of Columbus Avenue, and we drove toward our favorite dim sum shop in Chinatown. We picked up a mixture of delicacies; of course we both snuck a pork dumpling before entering the precinct.

"We bring gifts," I said as we walked toward Sokolov's desk.

"Abby, Kyle, what a wonderful greeting," he said as he took the box from my hands and placed it on his desk. "This is Detective Adrian Bennie."

"I've heard a lot about you two," Bennie said as he stood and extended his arm.

"What? You're listening to this big guy?" I said, motioning to Sokolov with my thumb.

"Sit. Sit." Sokolov gestured to a couple of chairs.

We all sat and then dug into the box.

"So why the gracious gift of food?" Sokolov asked in between chews.

"We needed to eat, and we also needed to talk to you about Suitcase Girl," Kang said.

"Is that what you've dubbed her over at the Bureau?"

"Not officially; it just made it easier to refer to her that way since we have no name."

"So the FBI *is* picking up the case?" Bennie asked before taking a large bite from a pork bao.

"We were able to pry some information from her during our visit at the hospital. From what we can tell, it's highly likely she was brought across state lines."

"Highly likely?" Bennie repeated.

I told them how our conversation took place and the connection Suitcase Girl had with me.

"Our supervisor has given us two days to dig around. To help expedite, I'm also housing her for those two days. She's my responsibility come tonight."

"From abandonment to abduction just like that," Bennie said. "My question now is why then stuff her in a piece of luggage and leave her on the doorstep of the largest law enforcement agency in this county?"

I shrugged. "I know, it doesn't quite track, but I think if we spend time poking around, we'll be able to answer that question."

"It's that damn suitcase," Kang said. "It has a way of throwing off every theory."

"The man that left her might have intended for her to be found dead," Sokolov reminded us.

"If that's the case, the suitcase could be a symbolic way to say goodbye," I said. "A father loses custody of the child. Kidnaps her. Realizes he won't ever be able to keep her. Starts to think if he can't have her, then no one can. Vengeance possibly?"

"A way to hurt his ex?" Bennie added.

Heads nodded as we mulled.

Sokolov broke the silence. "I appreciate the follow-up. You know the suitcase never sat well with me. But you understand, our hands..." He crossed his wrists in an X formation.

"Well, don't hold your breath. Depending on where this leads, there may be a task force on the horizon." I smiled.

Bennie handed a file to Kang. "That's everything we have. The suitcase is in the evidence locker. You can sign for it on the way out. The rape kit is at our crime lab, but you might want to have it transferred to your guys."

Kang and I both stood. "It's been fun, but we've got work to do."

"You'll keep us posted?" Sokolov inquired. His stare softened. He was genuinely interested in the case.

I popped one last dumpling into my mouth before delivering a wink and walking away.

CHAPTER SEVENTEEN

It was six in the evening when the doorbell rang. Exactly on cue, Lucy stopped setting the dinner table and sprinted toward the front door. Ever since she discovered that some people visit for the sole reason to sell us food, whether it be for a charity or a fundraiser, she wanted to be the one to answer the door and give her opinion first on whether to buy.

But I knew this wasn't the reason she had run to the door.

I had already prepped the family that we would have a guest staying with us. Lucy was excited because curiosity was her nature. Ryan thought it would be cool to have someone around the same age as he. Po Po, as I suspected, quickly changed parts of the menu that night to impress the new mouth.

"Hello," Lucy said, holding the door open.

I had already told her before never to blindly open the door. We were still working on that bad habit.

Rosales smiled and waved. "Hi. I hope we didn't come at a bad time," she said.

Suitcase Girl stood next to her, holding a paper grocery bag against her chest with both arms.

"No, don't be silly." I opened the door wider. "Come inside. We were just getting ready for dinner. You're welcome to join us, Christine."

"As lovely as it smells from here, I'm already late for dinner at my own home." She smiled warmly.

"Well, then. Let's hurry this along so you can get out of here."

"Lucy, why don't you go back in the kitchen and see if Po Po needs help?"

Rosales stepped inside with the girl. "Could you show me where she will be sleeping?"

"Yes, of course. We have a guestroom on the first floor. My mother in-law's room is next to it."

I led her down the hall. I was about to stop and make the introductions when I suddenly realized I didn't know the girl's actual name, and I wasn't about to introduce her as Suitcase Girl. So I continued past the kitchen and on to the guestroom. Once out of earshot of Po Po and Lucy, I whispered to Rosales if she or the shelter had given her a name.

"In my records, she's Jane Doe plus her case number. The shelter on the other hand refers to her as Jane."

"Does she respond to the name?"

"You know, I'm not sure. I always call the girls with no known name by 'Sweetie,' and if it's a boy, 'Tiger.' They seem to like that."

I opened the door to the bedroom. It was fairly basic: a full-size bed, a small dresser, and a bedside table with a lamp on it. There were some framed paintings of Chinese landscapes hanging on the wall, but that was about it for décor. Lucy had placed her favorite stuffed animal on the bed for Suitcase Girl—a panda she had named Dim Sum.

"This will be your new home for the next couple of days," Rosales said.

The girl stood quietly at the threshold. I placed a hand gently against her back and ushered her forward. "Do you like it?"

She looked up at me and smiled.

Rosales said, "The shelter provided her with a few items of clothing and toiletries. That's what's in the bag."

"Oh, okay. Well, maybe I'll take her shopping for more clothes."

After a quick tour of the house, Rosales removed paperwork from her handbag. "I'll need you to fill in the contact information and answer these questions, and then sign here and here. I prepared most of it in anticipation of me finding the place suitable."

It took about ten minutes for me to fill out the paperwork.

"Here's my card in case you need to reach me. I'll touch base later, and we can arrange a time for me to pick her up two days from now."

"Yup, sounds like a plan."

I walked her to the front door and said goodbye. After closing the door, I turned around to find Suitcase Girl standing behind me. She hesitated to look directly at me. I knelt down and smiled at her. "You don't have to be afraid. My family is very nice, and everyone is happy to have you here. Hmmm, but I do need to call you something. What name shall I give you?"

She shrugged.

I didn't want to call her Jane. So sanitary. As I struggled for a proper name, Po Po appeared, speaking Chinese. Dinner was ready.

"We need a name for her," I said.

Po Po looked at the little girl for a moment before saying, "Xiaolian."

Considering she was on the short side for her age. I thought it was appropriate.

"Do you like the name Xiaolian? It means 'little lotus.'"

The girl smiled.

"I want you to meet Po Po."

Po Po smiled and nodded at the girl. "She must be hungry," she said, continuing to speak in Chinese. She took the girl's hand. We usually spoke English in the house.

"Why aren't you speaking in English?" I asked as I followed them.

She stopped, lifted the girl's chin so she could look directly into her eyes. "Do you understand me?" she asked the girl in Chinese.

The girl nodded.

"She understand."

While I tried to comprehend what had just happened, Ryan appeared at the bottom of the stairs, freshly showered.

"Ryan, I want you to meet Xiaolian."

"Hi, nice to meet you," he said.

Xiaolian took a step behind Po Po, but kept her gaze on the floor.

"She's shy," I answered.

Dinner was already on the table, and Lucy sat in her seat with wide grin. "She can sit here." She patted the chair next to her. "My name is Lucy. Nice to meet you."

Xiaolian offered a meek smile as she took her seat. I had told everyone beforehand not to bombard her with questions and definitely not to ask her anything about her situation. I wanted

us to have a normal dinner, one no different than we have every
night.

And that was exactly what happened.

CHAPTER EIGHTEEN

AFTER DINNER, Ryan had some homework he needed to finish, so he headed back to his room on the second level. Po Po spoke on the phone with a friend. Lucy, Xiaolian, and I retired to the third floor to watch TV in the entertainment room until Lucy's bedtime—eight o'clock. Ryan's was at nine.

I had purposely waited until after Ryan and Lucy were tucked into bed before talking to Xiaolian. We returned to her room on the first floor. The shelter had provided her with pajamas. They were old but would suffice. After she had a quick shower, I tucked her into bed.

"Are you having fun?" I asked as I brought a chair over to the bed and sat.

She smiled sheepishly.

"You understand me?" I asked in Chinese.

She nodded.

I had to ask the next question. "Are you from China?"

She shrugged.

"Do you understand me?" I asked in English.

She nodded.

Very interesting. It wasn't something that surprised me tremendously though. Ryan and Lucy were bilingual. In fact, many Chinese children at their school spoke and understood both Chinese and English. *How did Po Po know?*

"Do you remember anything about where you are from? Or your mom and dad?"

She shook her head.

"Do you know the man who put you in the suitcase?"

"No," she said softly.

She speaks!

"Are you sure you don't know the man?"

She nodded.

"What do you remember?"

Her eyes fell to the side for a moment before she answered. "A man with a white coat."

"Were you in the hospital?"

She shrugged.

"But there were doctors?" I grabbed my phone and searched for an image of a doctor wearing a white coat. "Like this?" I showed her the photo.

She nodded.

"When we first met, you were in a hospital. Was the place you came from like that?"

She shook her head.

Hospitals can look different, but I had to imagine the interiors had similarities across the board. *An institution perhaps? I wonder...*

I made a mental note to check the local hospitals that care for children with psychiatric problems.

She yawned and her eyelids lowered.

"I know you're tired. We can talk more later." I gave her a

kiss on the forehead and then switched off the lamp on the bedside table.

As I closed her bedroom door behind me, I didn't hear any talking coming from Po Po's room. I figured she had gone to bed. I checked the lock on the rear door and then walked to the front door and checked the deadbolt. I switched off the lamp near the bay window and then looked out across my front lawn for a moment.

The moon that night shone bright, allowing me to see all the way over to my neighbor's house across the street. In front of their lawn was a parked car. At least I thought it was parked until the headlights suddenly turned on and it drove off. I thought nothing of it and headed upstairs to my room.

Later that night, I stirred in my sleep and, out of habit, checked the time on my phone. It was a little after three in the morning. I placed the phone back down. That was when I gasped

Xiaolian was standing at the foot of my bed.

I switched on a small lamp. "What's wrong, sweetie? Did you have a nightmare?"

The look on her face was a pretty good indicator that she had. I patted the bed. "Come here."

She climbed up on top and then slipped under the covers next to me.

"Do you want to tell me about your dream?"

She chewed on her bottom lip. "The girls," she said.

"Girls? Do you have sisters?"

"No."

"Who are these other girls?"

"I don't know."

"Don't know or don't remember?"

"I don't know them."

"But you were with them?"

"Yes."

"When were you with them?"

"Before I was found."

"Hmmm, were they Chinese?"

She nodded.

My first thought was she may have been trafficked into the country. Of course if that were the case, why then stuff her in a suitcase and dump her outside the FBI offices? My second thought was that she spoke English without a noticeable accent. If she were from China, she would have some accent, unless she was raised around English-speaking people.

I wonder...

When Po Po and I spoke Chinese with her, we did so in Cantonese. I asked in Mandarin if she understood me. She nodded.

"Do you remember flying on a plane?"

"No."

"What about driving in a car?"

"No."

"Were the other girls the same age as you?"

She shrugged.

"Did they look younger or older?"

"Older."

"How many were there?"

She shrugged again.

"Three? Ten? Twenty?"

"Not a lot."

"And you were with these girls before you were put in the suitcase?"

"Yes."

"Do you know if they were put in suitcases too?"

"I don't know."

"Did you try talking to them?"

"No, but I heard one crying."

"Heard? You didn't see them?"

"Only when the light came on."

"You were in a dark place and sometimes a light turned on?"

"Yes."

"Who turned on the light?"

She shrugged.

"You definitely heard crying in the dark?"

"Yes."

"Have you ever seen these girls before?"

"No."

"Are you sure?"

She nodded.

No planes. No cars. They were in a place where the lights were turned on and off but not by their control.

"Do you think you traveled?"

She thought for a moment. "We were moving."

I searched for an image of a typical eighteen-wheeler and showed her the picture. "Were you riding in a truck?"

She pointed at the long trailer. "This."

"This is familiar? You were in a container like this?"

"Yes."

"The other girls too?"

She nodded.

Well, that explained them having no control over the lighting situation. I made another mental note to check CCTV coverage of streets surrounding the office. It wouldn't be hard to spot a semi-truck driving around at three in the morning.

This investigation had quickly shaped up to be a case of human trafficking, but why would the traffickers leave her at the FBI offices? Were they trying to kill her? Did they think she was dead? It made no sense. Why not just dump the body if they believed she was dead? Did they want her to be found? What about the other girls? Did they drop them off at other places?

I made another mental note to expedite the rape kit. There was only one reason young Chinese girls were trafficked into this country: prostitution. I also knew the men operating these prostitution rings tended to sell the girls to other rings. It was a way to keep fresh faces for their customers. Girls could easily be passed on for years. Some escaped, some ended up dead, and many ended up drug addicts. Rarely did I hear of them being let go, but there were girls who were discarded when the pimps felt like there was no value in them. I wondered if these girls were at the end of their product cycle?

She yawned, pulling me out of my thought process, and cuddled into my side. Within seconds she fell asleep, and I had all the reasoning I needed to pursue the case.

CHAPTER NINETEEN

THE FOLLOWING morning I helped Xiaolian settle in at breakfast with the rest of the family before heading up to my home office on the third floor. Once there, I called Kang.

"How was the first night with Suitcase Girl?" he asked.

"I couldn't introduce her as Suitcase Girl, so I'm calling her Xiaolian."

"Little lotus, huh? That's much better."

"I made progress last night. She's speaking. Oh, guess what? You'll appreciate this. She understands Mandarin and Cantonese."

"Really?"

"Po Po spoke to her, and she totally understood her. Don't ask me why Po Po thought to speak Chinese to the girl, but she did. And when the girl speaks English, there isn't any noticeable accent. I imagine she's fluent in both Chinese and English."

"She's educated."

"Yup."

"Interesting."

"Yeah, but that language thing, while impressive, isn't the reason why I'm calling you. Turns out she's not the only one."

"What do you mean?"

"There were other Chinese girls with her. She said they were held in a dark container, most likely the trailer of a semi-truck."

"Trafficking?"

"Sounds like it, but she also mentioned a doctor, or at least a man in a white coat. I don't quite know how that fits."

"So she and a bunch of other girls were trafficked into the States from China."

"Yes, but if you bring the suitcase back into the picture..."

"I see what you're saying, Abby. Why ditch the merchandise, first of all? Secondly, why do it at the FBI offices?"

"Exactly, unless these girls have been in the States for a while and were considered unwanted goods by the ring. Even if that's true, why ditch the girl at our office? You see how the information wants to point toward trafficking, but the suitcase says otherwise?"

"I do." Kang let out a breath. "The good news is I think our case for taking on this investigation is growing stronger."

"Are you kidding me? It's a slam dunk."

"What can I do?" he asked.

"Expedite the rape kit. If she was here for a while, working... well, they might find something. Also, let's run the prints on the suitcase through every database we have access to. This ring may not be local. Also, have the lab check the inside and outside of the suitcase for DNA. One last thing, we need to look at CCTV footage of the surrounding street and see if a semi-truck rolled up to our offices that morning. Pull Hansen and Pratt in on this if you need to."

"Will do. I'm heading in now," Kang said.

"I'll be in a little later. I want to talk with her a bit more."

After the call, I headed back downstairs and joined everyone at the table. Xiaolian had made a nice dent in a healthy serving of Po Po's pancakes.

"Is it good?" I asked.

She grinned and nodded.

"Of course it good," Po Po quickly reaffirmed with a few tsks.

I saw that the pancakes were made with bananas so I munched on one, dry.

"Po Po, do you mind walking the kids to school today? I want to talk to Xiaolian for a bit before I go to work."

"Yes, I can."

A little later I said goodbye to Po Po and the kids. Xiaolian had taken a seat in the living room. I grabbed a pen and a small notepad and joined her.

"Are you having fun here?"

She nodded.

"I'm glad to hear that."

My priority that morning was to see if she could identify any of her captors or the truck they were riding in.

"I want to talk about the time you spent in the dark with the other girls. Is there anything you can tell me about the inside of this space? Was it cold? Was it hot? Did it smell funny?"

"No."

"No what?"

"It wasn't cold or hot. I had a blanket."

I jotted her answer down. "What about food or water?"

"We had food and water."

"Anything else you can remember about the truck? Did you

hear any strange noises? Did it stop for any extended period of time?

Xiaolian just stared at me.

"We'll come back to the truck later. The man who put you in the suitcase, do you remember what he looked like?"

She shrugged.

"What about his voice? Would you recognize it?"

She shrugged again. "Maybe."

"Was there more than one man?"

"Yes, there were three."

"Did these men speak English or Chinese?"

She nodded.

"They spoke both languages?"

"Uh-huh."

I found the same image of the semi-truck I had shown her last night. "Do you remember anything about the outside of the container? The color, or if there were words or pictures on it?"

"It was a light color."

"But no words or pictures?"

"No." She looked off to the side.

"Think hard. It's very important."

She closed her eyes for a moment and concentrated. A few moments later, she let out a defeated breath before opening her eyes.

"It's okay, sweetie. Maybe you'll remember later."

But she closed her eyes again, tighter this time. Suddenly she gasped and jerked her head. "I remember numbers."

"Okay, what were they?"

She rattled off four letters and seven digits.

"You remember all of that?"

She nodded.

I wasn't about to look a gift horse in the mouth. She had just provided me with a solid lead.

I called Kang and told him Xiaolian had identified the shipping code of the trailer. "There's got to be some way to track it down," I said.

"I'm sure there is. I'll get on it. Any chance it might be a logo or a name instead?"

"Looks like an identification code. I would start there, and if you feel like you need to cross-reference, do so. I'll be in soon to help."

The rest of my conversation with the girl went nowhere. It seemed that was the only real detail she could recall about the container. Same with the men and the doctor she had mentioned.

By then, Po Po had returned from the school. She had agreed earlier to watch Xiaolian while I went to work. I contemplated bringing her to the office, but I felt the progress we made was connected with her staying at my home. I didn't want to screw it up.

"I might swing by during lunch to talk to her again," I said to Po Po. "I'll call beforehand."

CHAPTER TWENTY

When I arrived, Kang was already at his desk talking on the phone.

"Good news?" I whispered as I removed my jacket and draped it over the back of my chair.

"More like no news," he said as he hung up. "There is a standard numeration on trailers, but it differs depending on the type of shipping container it is. We also need to factor in if it's independent or company owned. If it's part of a drop-container program, then hundreds of different companies will have access to it. Worst-case scenario is that it's independently owned. It'll be hard to track. The numbers might even be fake."

"So this will take time," I said.

He nodded. "Finding that container would help make our case to Reilly."

"I'll be back."

I walked over to where Hansen and Pratt sat at their desks. "What are you guys working on?"

"We have the lab expediting the rape kit and combing the suitcase for DNA. We're already running her prints and picture through the NCIC. If there's DNA, we'll move on that as well. We also have a request in to the city for access to their CCTV cameras that cover the streets surrounding our building. We were just about to head out and see if there are any cameras owned by private businesses, like a convenience store. They usually have cameras outside their premises. It's faster to ask them to check their footage than to cut through the red tape with the city."

"Hold off on that for now. I need you two to help on something else."

"Whatever you need, we're in."

I filled them in on the identification number that Xiaolian recalled and set them loose.

"Are they in?" Kang asked when I returned.

"Yeah, that'll free you up."

Kang and I talked a bit about what I had learned that morning and the previous night.

"The doctor..." Kang scratched his chin. "Maybe it's nothing more than for health reasons. You know, to check for pregnancies or STDs."

"Could be, if they had plans to sell the girls to another ring."

"Of course if we introduce the suitcase back into the picture—"

"I know, I know. It doesn't jibe with the trafficking angle." I leaned back in my chair and slouched.

"Maybe what Sokolov said earlier was true," Kang proposed.

"What? That she should have been found dead?" I crossed my arms over my chest and let out a breath while I mulled the possibility.

"Yeah, maybe she wasn't working out so well and they decided to get rid of her."

"If that's really the case, they could have dumped her anywhere. Why at our offices?"

"Million-dollar question, right?" Kang scratched his cheek.

"I also find it hard to believe that these guys tried to kill her by injecting a sedative in her body. It's a bit sophisticated. A gunshot to the head I would buy. Feeding her enough drugs so she overdoses, sure. But propofol?"

"So it was to calm not to kill?"

"Would you willingly let someone lock you inside of a suitcase?"

"Not a chance in hell."

"You know." I wagged my finger at Kang. "I think we're coming at the suitcase the wrong way."

"How so?"

"We keep asking why they left her. Maybe they *wanted* us to find her."

CHAPTER TWENTY-ONE

REILLY REMOVED HIS GLASSES, placed them on his desk, and rubbed his eyes. "Let me see if I got this straight. You're saying the person who did this to the girl wanted us to find her. Wait, strike that... *investigate* her."

"That's exactly what I'm saying. We kept thinking it was the trafficking ring that left the girl, but what if it wasn't the trafficking ring? What if it was a person who had no connection with them?"

"Someone who wants to take down the ring? A vigilante?" Reilly questioned.

"That's a possibility. We don't know the connection as of yet, but it's the only way we can plausibly fit the suitcase into all of this."

"Look, based on what you've discovered, I'm inclined to think the same. Suitcase Girl is—"

"Her name's Xiaolian."

"... It appears that Xiaolian was trafficked, along with a bunch of other girls. She may have escaped or perhaps a customer felt sympathetic and helped her escape but didn't want to get more involved, so he dumps her outside our office."

"That's a scenario that works."

"Where are you guys on finding this mystery tractor trailer?"

"We're digging. I have Hansen and Pratt helping."

"Housing that girl paid off, Abby."

"Every time we speak, she remembers a bit more. Slowly this puzzle is putting itself together."

Reilly slipped his glasses back on. "All right, the two-day restriction is lifted for now, but I want daily updates."

We were just standing up when Hansen suddenly appeared outside Reilly's door.

"Good news. We figured out the problem with that tracking number. It's not associated with tractor trailers. That's a standard identification number associated with cargo containers." Hansen held up a tablet with the number on the screen. "The first three letters identify the owner, the next one identifies the type of container, and the numbers essentially identify that specific container."

"Cargo containers are long and narrow like a tractor trailer," Kang said. "Easy mistake for the girl to make."

"So, wait, that means they were aboard a cargo ship?" I asked.

"Yes and no," Hansen said. "Cargo containers are a standard shape, so not only can they be stacked on any ship, they can also be loaded on trains and hauled by semi-trucks."

"Traveling across the ocean in a cargo container?" Reilly mused. "How is that even possible?"

"Maybe it's a cargo container being hauled by a truck," I said. "Maybe that's just how they were transported over land."

"If the last thing she remembered before being put in the suitcase was being in that container, it could be any of the three scenarios: a truck, a train, or a ship," Hansen said. "Cargo ships are offloaded in the Port of Oakland. Union Pacific Railway also has a transloading terminal in Oakland, as well as in South San Francisco and in Richmond."

"So a truck could have been her final transport to our offices that morning."

"Technically, yes, but we just learned that trucks hauling tractor trailers are usually longer than sixty-five feet. To drive within the city, they're required to have an extralegal truck permit. Also, most of the streets in the surrounding area restrict commercial vehicles over three tons."

"So she was transferred from the container to another vehicle and then transported to our offices."

"Most likely that's what happened. Pratt is already on the phone with the Port of Oakland to see if that container arrived there via a cargo ship."

"I'll get on the phone with Union Pacific and see if they offloaded the container there," I said. "Hansen, you handle the railroad terminal in Richmond. Kyle, South San Francisco rail-road terminal is yours."

We hurried out of Reilly's office and back to our desks. Pratt was still on the phone when I saw him. He waved me over to his desk.

"Yes, that's correct. Do not let that ship leave," he said to the person on the other end of the line. "I understand, but there is a container aboard that is a part of a federal criminal investiga-tion." He wrote the dock number and other information down on a piece of paper. "We're on our way." He hung up his phone.

"The number checks out. That container is on a ship about to leave the port and head back to China."

I glanced at my watch. "If traffic plays nice, it'll take us at least forty-five minutes to get there."

"There's a Customs and Border Protection office there," Pratt said.

"Call them, see if they can help stop that ship."

"I have a contact with SFPD's Marine Unit," Kang said. "I'm not sure what they're capable of, but if push comes to shove, I bet they can have their boats block the exit of the bay."

I grabbed my cell phone from my desk and dialed Agent House at the Oakland FBI Field Office. "Yes, that's right. Agent Hansen will text you all the information; we're also notifying Border Protection. We're on our way. Just make sure that ship doesn't leave." I turned to Kang. "House is heading over there now."

"What do you want us to do?" Pratt asked as he stood next to Hansen.

"Call the garage for an SUV. You two are coming with us. This investigation is officially a go."

CHAPTER TWENTY-TWO

Agent Frankie Ray with US Customs and Border Protection met us at the main entry gates to the port. He waved at us with squinty eyes as he walked over to our vehicle.

"I'll ride with you, if that's all right," he said, peeking in through the window. He eased himself into the back seat and, once settled, gave us directions. "We're heading to the Charles P. Howard Terminal. So just follow this road for now."

"Do you often have to turn a ship around?" I asked.

"No, it's a big deal to do that. If we have questions or concerns regarding cargo, we flag it immediately and notify the captain and crew. At that point, nothing is unloaded or loaded until we say so. I pulled a file on that ship. It's an independent freighter. The name is *Hong Long*."

"That means 'red dragon,'" Kang said.

"This isn't the ship's first visit to the port. It's had numerous visits over the last three years. Turn left up here," Ray pointed. "It arrived in our port two days ago. According to the shipping manifest, the container held a mix of consumer goods: electronics, toys, appliances, and clothing. There were also a fair amount of dry and perishable goods. Average turnaround time for a typical vessel is two to three days, but this ship wasn't that big so it barely took two days."

"Do you know if the container was empty when it was loaded back on?"

"According to the manifest, it is. You guys were lucky. Just a couple of hours later and the ship would have been out of the bay and in international waters. It's my understanding that you believe the cargo container in question was used for the purposes of human trafficking?"

"That's correct," I said.

"I'd be surprised if it were true. The conditions in the containers can fluctuate widely out on the open ocean. Then there's the question of basic necessities like food and water. The ship had a stop in Hawaii, but even the journey from there to Oakland is a week and a half. It's a long time to be cooped up."

"I'm assuming you can't inspect every cargo container that comes through here."

"You're absolutely right. The Port of Oakland can handle any ship, and we get all kinds. Ninety-nine percent of all containerized goods moving through Northern California are loaded and discharged here. The way we prioritize our inspections is by looking at the cargo manifest, the past history of the ship or the company that owns it, tips we receive, and lastly, our gut instinct. Keep driving straight. The berth is just up ahead."

"No red flags obviously with this cargo ship."

"Nope, but I'm extremely interested in seeing this container. We try to learn from every experience."

Containers stacked four high covered most of the dock with the exception of the area near the docked ships. Agent House was leaning against her vehicle when we arrived.

"That's the container," she said, pointing upward.

A cream-colored steel box was locked in the claw of a container crane and moving slowly above us. A stevedore with his neck cocked back radioed instructions to the operator.

All eyes followed the path of the container. We had no idea what, if anything, we would find inside of it. I just knew the number stenciled on the outside matched the number Xiaolian had given me.

The container was forty-feet long, eight-feet wide, and six-feet tall. Aside from the identification number, there were no other markings. No company name or logo. Nothing.

The container touched down on the pavement. A couple of longshoremen quickly unhooked the four cables securing the container to the claw. One gave the operator of the crane the thumbs-up.

A black lockbox secured the front door of the container, and the stevedore asked one of the longshoreman to retrieve a bolt cutter. Minutes seemed like hours as we waited. Kang stood next to me and kept dipping his hands in and out of the front pockets of his slacks.

"Would you stop fidgeting?" I whispered. "You're making me nervous."

"Sorry, it's just that we know it's empty, so I'm wondering what is it we hope to find."

"Answers," I said.

The longshoreman returned and quickly snipped the lock off before pulling the door wide open and revealing the inside.

No one moved.

We just stared.

Even Agent Ray stood dumbfounded. "I've never seen

anything like this." He was the first to say anything as he took a step forward.

We all did the same for a better look. From what we could tell from the outside looking in, the container appeared to have been transformed into a highly sophisticated living space. I saw bunk beds, chairs, a refrigerator... There were even a few stacked cases of bottled water and dry food.

Agent Ray called for backup from his agency. They would take the lead on questioning the captain and crew, and we were to handle the longshoremen involved with unloading the container. We agreed to reconvene later and share what was learned.

The stevedore in charge introduced himself. "My name's Neil Tate. I've radioed the office for a list of the men who were assigned to the unloading of the ship." Just then, a voice on the other end of the radio rattled off a few names and said those men were on their way to his location.

"Not everyone is working today," he said.

"That's fine, we'll question the ones here. It shouldn't take very long. If you could compile the contact information for the others, we'll reach out to them ourselves."

"Sure, no problem."

One by one, men appeared wearing yellow hard hats, jeans, and long- or short-sleeve shirts with red reflective safety vests over them. Hansen and Pratt took the first two. House and Kang took the next two. The last one came from another direction, from behind a few stacked containers.

"That's the last one," Tate said, pointing.

When the man's eyes met with mine, he literally stopped in his tracks.

You're going to run, aren't you?

He did.

"We got a runner!" I shouted out as I took off after him.

Kang and the rest of my crew were right behind me as I ran into the maze of containers.

"Spread out," I shouted. "Try to flank him."

He was heavyset—no way he could outrun me. Even with numerous left and right turns, I closed the gap with each step. Down a narrow pathway he ran, where the containers were stacked even higher, eliminating any direct sunlight.

"FBI!" I shouted. "Stop now!"

He glanced back. Fear shot from his eyes. But he didn't stop. In fact, it seemed he ran faster. Up ahead was a T intersection.

Which way are you turning?

He turned left.

A second later, Kang appeared from the right of the intersection like a speeding bullet. He had his arms stretched out as he leaned in with his shoulder. He hit the guy from behind with such force they both were airborne for a few feet before hitting the pavement hard.

When I caught up, I slammed my knee straight into the guy's back, pinning him facedown. Within seconds, I had his hands cuffed securely behind his back.

"Nice hit," I said as I helped Kang to his feet.

"I played defensive tackle in high school." He smiled and brushed his hands together. "His blindside was wide open."

The runner's name was Carlos Medina. I had him kneel next to our vehicle. He was still breathing heavily, and a ring of sweat had soaked the collar of his shirt.

Kang and the other agents had returned to finish questioning their men.

"Why did you run?"

"I need the exercise."

"You see that container over there? Two nights ago it was unloaded from a ship named the *Hong Long*. Your supervisor tells me you were the forklift operator who moved it to the holding location."

"Yeah, so? That's my job. I move a lot of containers. This is a shipyard. What do you expect?"

"According to the manifest, this container was supposed to be carrying a bunch of consumer goods and food."

"Yeah, so?"

I folded my arms across my chest. "Funny thing is, it wasn't. Instead, it was used to smuggle underage Chinese girls into the US for the purposes of sex. You know what the federal sentencing is for human trafficking? The trafficking of a minor alone is a minimum of four years. We're pretty sure some sort of rape charge can be added, so that's probably another nine years. Add in kidnapping and prostitution of a minor—another ten years. Of course if we can prove kidnapping to commit sexual crimes with a minor... Wow, that's life in prison. Talk about a life-changing experience."

Medina avoided my eyes as he chewed on his bottom lip and continuously wiped the streams of perspiration running down his face with his shoulder.

"That's a lot of time for one victim, which we have already identified. In the next hour or so, my forensics team will start working on that container. They'll find DNA, and we'll identify the other girls who were in there. That's really when the time will start to add up for you. Are you hearing all of this?"

"I have no idea what you're talking about. I didn't kidnap or traffic any girls. All I did was move the container."

I shifted my weight to one foot and shook my head slowly.

"I'm really having a hard time believing you right now, because earlier, you and I," I pointed at him then at myself, "we had a moment. Remember making eye contact and then running away? Sure you do. But if it helps, I wasn't the only one who noticed. Four other FBI agents noticed, as did the agent with Customs and Border Protection, your boss, and your coworkers. That's a lot of people testifying against you."

"I'm telling you, I didn't do anything," Medina said with a raised voice.

"Well, if I'm wrong, that would be a travesty for you to take the fall for crimes you didn't commit. A damn travesty." I scrunched down and whispered in his ear. "But that's what will happen. Believe me when I say that."

CHAPTER TWENTY-THREE

I LEFT Medina alone for a bit so his imagination could run wild as he pondered his fate. Kang had just finished questioning his guy.

I bounced my eyebrows at him. "Anything?"

"He remembers unloading the container but says that's all he did... said your guy was the forklift operator that hauled it away after telling him he could handle it on his own. I don't think my guy knew what was in that container."

Hansen and Pratt had received the same answers from the men they questioned, and so had House. I filled them in on my conversation with Medina. "He could very well be working alone. Hansen, Pratt, I want you two to pull records for every visit the *Hong Long* has made to port. See if this container was on board, and if it was, find out the name of the forklift operator. Also, Agent Ray mentioned this ship docked in Hawaii. Reach out to our field office there and see if they can poke around. Someone probably helped there as well, maybe checked on the girls or provided a new supply of food and water."

"I've already alerted CSI," House said. "You want me to oversee that?"

"I do. In fact, this investigation has task force written all over it, but the upside is we have an opportunity to take down a large ring, maybe more. Customs is now part of this growing task force. We need a command center where everyone can play nice together."

House chuckled. "Wishful thinking but I'll get that set up. We can have the container moved to a secure facility in the SOMA area where forensics can get to work. The place is big enough to act as our command center too."

Kang and I walked back over to Medina.

"Hey, my knees are killing me," he whined.

"Too bad. Remember him?" I pointed my thumb at Kang.

"I'm Agent Kang. I understand you're volunteering to take credit for this entire operation. You need some serious *cojones* to do that. Inside federal prison, the lowest man on the totem pole is the one convicted for preying on minors. I hear the stories." Kang's body shivered. "Makes my stomach turn."

Medina licked his lips. His eyes darted all over the place, probably searching for an exit from the mess he found himself in. There were none.

"Are you trying to think up a new story?" I asked. "It might be a little too late for that. Your pals who were with you the night that container was unloaded... they all said you drove off in one direction and they headed in another. You told them to go home so you could be alone... because you needed to let the girls out."

"That's not true."

"We think it is."

"It's amazing how the kingpin of an organization never looks like a kingpin," Kang said.

"Kingpin? I'm not in charge of anything. I just work for them."

A smile formed on my face. "A second ago you claimed to have had nothing to do with it. Now you're admitting to working for someone. If you don't start telling us everything right now, you will take the heat for this. I guarantee it."

"Okay, okay. About a year and a half ago, I'm getting into my car after a shift and this guy approaches me."

"Did you know him or see him before?"

"Never."

"This guy have a name?"

"He never mentioned one. Didn't even want to know my name."

"What did he look like?"

"Hard to tell. It was dark the first night I met him. Plus he was dressed in black, had a hoodie and sunglasses. Every time I met with him after that, he always dressed the same way. But he was young."

"How do you know?"

"The way his voice sounded, and the parts of his face I did see looked young. I really didn't want to know much. I knew this was fishy stuff, so I felt the less I knew the better, right?"

"Okay, so some guy you don't know or even recognize approaches you after a shift, then what?"

"He asked me if I wanted to make some easy money. At the time, I was in a real bind financially. So I said I was interested. He goes on to tell me that every so often he would have a shipment arriving on a cargo ship. All he wanted me to do was to move the container to an area where he could unload the goods into a couple of vans. He said the entire thing would take fifteen minutes tops, and he would pay me five thousand dollars."

"Did you see what it was he unloaded?"

"Well, yeah. Each time it was a bunch of girls."

"How many times did you do this for him?"

"This was the third time."

"So he would contact you with the shipping information, you would then set aside the container for him, and he would show up later and load the girls into these vans?"

"Yeah, two vans actually. He was always waiting nearby, because after I texted him that I had the container in the spot, he would show up a few minutes later. He would load up the girls, and they would be gone."

"They? More than one guy showed up?"

Xiaolian did mention three men.

"Yeah, there were four, but they all dressed the same: black jeans, black hoodie. Ray Bans. But I could tell one was a girl just by the way her body looked. She had curves."

"Did you see the inside of the container?" Kang asked.

"Nah, I always stayed seated in my forklift off to the side. I didn't want to see any more than needed. In fact, I made it a point to look away."

"So after they loaded the girls into the vehicles, what happened?"

"One of them hands me an envelope with five thousand dollars in it. They go their way. I go my way."

"Do you have this person's phone number?"

"Sure, but each time he contacts me, it's from a different number."

"How is it they are able to drive in and out? There's a security gate."

"There's another gate here that leads directly to Market Street. It's mostly used by people who work here."

"So which security guard is on your contact's payroll?"

Medina let out a breath. "Corey Watts."

"Anybody else working here involved with this operation?"

"As far as I know it's just us two. I don't even think I'm supposed to know about him. They never told me, but I happened to see the guy talking to Corey on his way out. I don't think Corey even knows I'm involved."

"You two never talked about it?"

"No way. I told you, I didn't want to know any more than necessary for me to do my part of the job."

CHAPTER TWENTY-FOUR

Corey Watts wasn't scheduled for a shift that day, but his apartment was near the corner of Filbert and 7th Street, about a five- to-ten-minute drive from the port. Kang and I took the drive over there.

"I'll be interested to see what forensics finds in that container," Kang said.

"There'll be a lot of DNA, that's for sure, but I'm not so sure how much it'll help us. Those girls most likely won't be in our database. Finding them would be much better."

Kang glanced over at me. "I'll tell you, though, that container seems like it's got everything needed for a journey overseas. Agent Ray mentioned it might even be equipped with a customized climate control system, one that's modified to deal with humans and not just perishables. This doesn't sound like your typical trafficking operation."

"I wonder if the smugglers are a separate organization from the prostitution ring."

"Usually the prostitution ring obtains their own girls, sort of the cost of doing business. But what you're saying could be a possibility."

"I was thinking it could be an answer for the suitcase. What if she was a separate delivery? Intended for someone else and not a prostitution ring?"

Kang pushed his bottom lip up as he thought about my theory. "So someone else takes Xiaolian. If we remove the other girls from the equation, it makes sense. It doesn't answer why they dropped her off at our office, but it explains why she was the only one."

"This is the address," I said, pointing ahead.

Watts's apartment was located on the second floor of a three-story building. Kang stood off to one side of the door. I stood on the other side. We could clearly hear the television inside.

"Corey Watts. This is the FBI. We'd like to ask you a few questions." I waited a beat for an answer before repeating myself.

Again, no one responded.

I checked the doorknob; it was unlocked. I shrugged and opened the door.

Sitting directly in front of us on a couch was a man engrossed with a show on killer whales.

"Are you Corey Watts?" I asked.

He placed a finger against his lips and then pointed at the television. Kang promptly walked over to the set and turned it off.

"Hey, man. Why'd you go and do that for?"

"Are you Corey Watts?"

"Yeah, man. Who's asking?"

I removed my identification. "I'm Agent Kane, and this is

Agent Kang. We're with the FBI. We want to ask you a few questions."

"Well, shit, man, you could have just knocked instead of barging in here and shutting my TV off."

"We did knock."

He scratched the back of his head. "You did?"

Kang picked up a plastic bag from off of the coffee table and shook the contents inside. "Are you high?"

"Hey, man, it's for medical purposes. I swear. I got a card and all."

"Mr. Watts, do you know a Mr. Carlos Medina?"

"The name sounds familiar. Is he in trouble?"

"He is and so are you. He fingered you as part of a gang that's smuggling underage girls into the US."

"What? That's crazy talk, man. I don't know nothing about smuggling any females."

"First off, I'm not your man. Second, he ID'd you as the guard who lets a group of individuals into the port—three men and a woman. They're all dressed in black and wear dark sunglasses."

"Oh, them. They pay me money to let them in, but that ain't smuggling."

"We believe those individuals are part of a smuggling ring. That makes you an accessory."

"Whoa, I admit I took the money and all, but I swear I didn't know nothing about this smuggling you're talking about."

"What did you think they were doing?"

"They just told me they needed to get in, grab some goods, and then get out. Fifteen, twenty minutes max. That's it."

"And this didn't strike you as something that could be illegal?"

"Man, oh excuse me, miss, I just thought it was something small, like maybe some counterfeit crap, since it came from China."

"What makes you think the stuff they wanted came from China?"

"Because they looked Asian. I figured their cousin or something hooked them up."

"Can you identify any of them?"

He shook his head. "Nah, they always wore them shades, but I could tell they was Asian. I had an Asian girlfriend before like you. If you was wearing shades, I'd still know you was Asian. You too," he said, pointing at Kang.

"So as far as you could tell, they were all Asian?" I asked.

"Positive."

"Did any of them have any distinguishing marks, like a Mohawk haircut or a tattoo or a scar on their face?"

"Nah, they always had their hoodies pulled over tight, their arms were covered, and they wore gloves."

"Can you identify the vehicle they drove?"

"Same each time. Two black vans."

"Right. Anything notable about these vans?"

"Nothing special about them except the paint job was crap."

"How so?"

"It was like they painted them with spray paint from a can. They had a dull color. Or maybe it was that black paint that professionals use, what's it called…" Watts snapped his finger repeatedly.

"An undercoat," Kang said.

"Yeah, that's it."

"And when they drove out, you weren't able to see anything inside the vans?"

"Nah, the windows were tinted, and they only rolled them down halfway. I could see inside through the front window but not into the back of the van."

"How do they notify you when they need to make a pickup?"

"They call me. I got the number."

Watts hesitated as he reached for a cell phone on the coffee table. I nodded that it was okay to grab it.

"This is the number they called me from a couple of days ago."

He turned the phone around so we could see the number. Kang snapped a photo of it with his phone.

"They always call about a week before the day they need access, so I know to make sure I'm working. About an hour before they show up, they call again and then once more about ten minutes before they come."

"Same number each time?"

"No, they change it, but that number might still be good."

"Call them," I said.

"What? I ain't got no reason to call them. They'll think something's up."

"They pay you in cash?"

"Crisp one-hundred dollar bills every time."

"Tell them they shorted you a hundred."

Watts shifted in his seat and licked his lips. "I don't know if that's a good idea—"

"I'm not asking you. I'm telling you. Now call."

"Man…" Watts dialed the number with a pout. "It's ringing." A few seconds later, he pulled the phone away from his ear. "No one's picking up."

I could hear the ringing.

"You want me to keep trying?"

"You can disconnect the call and then you can stand up," I said.

Kang produced a pair of handcuffs. "Turn around and place your hands behind your back."

"Why? I told you everything. I cooperated."

"And we appreciate it," he said, "but we're still arresting you."

It was nearly five p.m. when we returned to the FBI offices. We were in with Reilly, updating him on everything.

"That sounds like an impressive container. Good job," he said.

"There's probably more we'll discover about it when the techs are finished. So far everything the girl has told us checks out."

"So we have an unspecified number of girls who were smuggled into the States via a cargo ship originating from Taiwan. It made one stop in Hawaii before coming here. Any reason to believe the girls aren't from Hawaii?"

"Well, Xiaolian looks Chinese and speaks the language. So we're assuming she's either from China or Taiwan. I'm hoping she'll eventually be able to remember more about the other girls."

"As it stands, you're now working with the theory that a prostitution ring and traffickers are involved and they may or may not be associated with each other?"

"It's a thought. It's the only way we can make sense of the

suitcase. Why let one girl go but not the others, unless the shipment was intended for multiple customers?"

Reilly nodded in agreement. "My experience with traffickers is that they spook easily. If they even get a slight hint that
someone in the chain has been pinched, they'll close up shop.
Make sure you guys stay on top of the other agencies involved
and that they don't go rogue. In fact, do your best to keep the
number of players involved to a minimum."

"From what we've gathered so far, the shipments come once
every six months, so we should be able to keep the investigation
contained," I said. "We're switching our efforts to finding those
other girls and identifying the players involved in the Bay Area.
That might lead to someone in Taiwan."

"We don't have an embassy in Taiwan," Reilly said. "We
have an agent stationed at the Hong Kong Embassy. I'll put in a
request to have that person quietly dig around. Keep me
posted."

CHAPTER TWENTY-FIVE

As soon as we were done with Reilly, I headed home. I was
eager to resume my conversation with Xiaolian. Dinner was
fairly normal; she seemed to have acclimated pretty quickly to
living with us. Overall she still remained on the quiet side, rele-
gating herself to being a listener; however, she had moved
beyond using head movements to communicate with Po Po and
the kids.

After dinner I asked Xiaolian to sit with me in the screened-
in porch at the back of the house. I placed two cups of tea on a
small table, and we sat on the rattan loveseat next to it.

"Are you having fun here?" I asked.

"Yes." She smiled at me.

"Is it like your home?"

"No, it's different."

"How is it different?"

"It just is."

"I want to show you something." I pulled up the pictures of
the container on my cell phone.

She drew a fast breath.

"You recognize it?"

"You found it?"

"Yes, but the other girls are still missing. I'm worried about them."

She looked closer at the picture. "This was my bed," she said, pointing to one of the bunks. "And this is where the food was kept cold. And that was a bathroom."

Her memory was returning, and so was her vocabulary.

"You had a bathroom?"

"Yes, we had everything." She cocked her head to the side. "Why?"

"Were you aware that you were on a ship?"

"Not at first. I woke up in there."

"You don't remember being put inside?"

She shook her head before turning away.

"How did you know you were on a ship?"

"I heard one of the others talk about it."

I took a sip of my tea. "Was it hot inside there?"

"There was an air conditioner that kept the temperature perfect."

"Really?"

"But we couldn't control it. It was automatic."

"And what about the lights?"

"They were automatic too. We had to use a flashlight if we wanted to go to the bathroom late at night."

"Do you know how long you were in there?"

She let out a breath as her gaze looked beyond the screen. "A while. It seemed like forever."

"Did you speak to the other girls?"

"Not really. Some of the girls talked to each other. One of the girls cried the whole time."

"Had you ever seen those girls before?"

"No.

"Beside sleeping and eating, what else did you do?"

"There were tablets we could watch movies on."

"And what happened when the battery went dead?"

"We had a charger."

Electricity? Whoever built this container put a lot of thought into the construction. I'm surprised they didn't have a shower. Wait...

"Did you guys have a shower?"

"No, we had plastic containers with wet cloths inside. I don't know what they're called, but it helped a little to keep us clean until they ran out." Xiaolian blew on her tea before taking a sip.

"They're called wet wipes. Let's talk about what happened when the doors to the container were opened. Tell me everything you remember."

"Which time?"

"The container was opened more than once?"

She nodded. "The first time it was at night outside. Two men came in with more food and water. They emptied the toilet and filled up the water container."

"Did they say anything? How long did all this take?"

"They didn't say anything at first, but the girl who was crying cried louder, and one of them hit her hard. We were scared, so no one said anything. They weren't there very long."

That must have taken place during the ship's stop in Honolulu. Supply refresh.

"Were you able to see what these men looked like?"

"They looked Chinese, but they had dark skin."

"Did they speak Chinese?"

"When they talked to us, they spoke Chinese, but I heard them speak English to each other."

"And the second time the container was opened, you were let out, right?"

"I remember I was sleeping and then I woke up."

"Someone woke you up."

"No, the container moved, like something jerked it hard. And then it felt like it was moving."

"You didn't hear anything?"

"No, we couldn't hear anything outside. Then the door opened, and two men came inside. They told us it was time to go."

"So when you were finally outside, what did you see?"

"Not much, I kept my head down. I was scared. Two people shined a flashlight in my face, and then looked at a piece of paper. They told me to wait by them. After that, they made me climb into a van."

"Are you sure there were only three men? That's what you told me earlier."

"Oh, no. There were four. I remember now."

"You didn't see a fifth person? A fat man on a forklift?"

"No. I'm sorry."

"It's okay, sweetie. You've done nothing wrong."

I already knew from Medina that the girls had been separated into the two vans, but I wanted to see if Xiaolian would confirm that.

"Did they put you and the other girls in one van?"

She shook her head. "There wasn't enough room in the van. Me and two girls were put in another van."

"Can you describe their faces?"

"It was too dark."

"What about their voices? Anything weird about the way they spoke?"

"Not really."

"Did they talk about where you were going or mention a direction or place?"

She shook her head and then reached for her cup of tea. I did the same. Everything Xiaolian had told me thus far matched with what Medina had told me. They corroborated each other. It seemed I had a pretty good understanding of how they'd arrived into the country. What I lacked was information on who ran the smuggling ring and where the other girls had been taken.

We sat alone with our thoughts for a moment or so. Mine were busy processing everything Xiaolian had relayed to me that night and what the next steps would be. I couldn't be sure what had her mind occupied. Maybe she wasn't thinking about anything and was simply content to be drinking her tea.

"When you were inside the van, did you still keep your head down?"

"Yes."

"Do you remember at any time one of the men giving you medicine, maybe an injection?"

She started to shake her head "no" but stopped. "Yes, one of the men did this. I forgot about that."

"Did you start to feel tired after?"

"Yes. How do you know they did that?"

"The doctors at the hospital found a sedative in your blood. It's a drug that makes you very sleepy."

"I had a hard time staying awake."

She yawned, triggering me to do the same. I was about to call it a night when she suddenly gasped.

"What is it?" My heartbeat sped up.

"I remember something. One man had a tattoo."

CHAPTER TWENTY-SIX

LATER THAT NIGHT, Xiaolian lay in bed, tossing and turning.

She's walking down a familiar narrow hallway. A man in a white coat is leading her. She still can't see his face.

"Hurry, we're late," he says.

He grabs her arm and hurries her along.

Another image appears. Suddenly she's outdoors sitting in a garden. It's peaceful. The sun is out, but a large rose apple tree shades her. Birds can be heard. A nearby water fountain babbles.

Another image populates her mind. This time she is in a room with white walls and no windows. She's sitting at a small rectangular table. There is no other furniture. There's a door but no handle.

She hears a voice. It's the same man who walked with her in the hall. It's coming from a lone speaker hanging in the corner of the room. In another corner, there is a surveillance camera. In fact, there are two of them.

"Are you ready?" the voice asks.

She nods.

"A man works on the thirty-eighth floor of an office building.

Everyday he takes the elevator to the lobby. He exits the building and walks to a nearby food stall, where he purchases and consumes their daily special for lunch. After he's finished, he returns to his building and enters the elevator. If there is someone else in the elevator or if it has been raining that day, he rides it back up to the thirty-eighth floor. If neither of those two variables occurs, he rides the elevator to the twentieth floor and then takes the stairs. Why? The clock has started."

She sits there for a moment.

"Time is wasting," the man's voice echoes.

"He's short," she finally says. "He can't reach any of the buttons above the twentieth floor but if he has an umbrella, or if someone else is in the elevator with him, then the button for the thirty-eighth floor can be pressed."

For a brief moment there's silence. The speaker crackles and the man speaks, but with much more force this time.

"A man and a woman are in a truck. They are speeding recklessly down a street. The vehicle screeches to a stop. The driver exits the truck and runs off. A few moments later he returns with another person. The woman in the passenger seat is now dead. Why?"

She takes a moment to think, but not as long as the last time. "They arrived at a hospital. By the time the man returned with a doctor, the lady was dead. Too late."

The man on the speaker is shouting and speaking faster.

"A woman is in court. She tells a judge that her sister murdered her husband. The sister claims she was never at the scene of the crime and it's her sister's word over hers and therefore the evidence isn't strong enough. The judge disagrees and tells her this is one instance where one person's word can single-handedly trump the other's."

There is no debating this time. She answers immediately "The women are Siamese twins." *She pounds the table with her fist. "Challenge me for once!"*

Xiaolian's eyes flickered open as she drew a quick breath, her body growing tense. For a brief moment she'd forgotten where she was, but then her memory returned. The rise and fall of her chest eased, and the muscles in her legs relaxed as she settled into the mattress. A tear escaped her eye.

CHAPTER TWENTY-SEVEN

THE NEXT MORNING, Kang and I made plans to carpool to the command center. I was in the middle of breakfast with the kids when he arrived.

"I'm a bit early," he said, standing on my porch.

I waved him inside. "Not a worry, I..."

"Something wrong?" he asked as he turned around to see what had me craning my neck.

"That car parked across the street, I think I saw it the night I brought Xiaolian home."

The engine started, and we watched it drive off.

"You sure?"

"No, I'm not sure. The shape looks similar. It's probably nothing." I shut the door. "Come on. Everyone's in the dining room."

"Hi, Uncle Kyle," my kids said in unison.

"Lucy, you're growing taller by the day. Ryan, how's your kung fu coming along?"

He flashed Kang the thumbs-up as he worked on a large mouthful.

"Grab a bite. There's plenty because of who's cooking."

"Silver dollars, my favorite. Nobody makes them like you do, Po Po."

He gave her a kiss on her forehead, and she smiled.

What a kiss butt.

"Sit, sit," Po Po said as she pulled a chair away from the table.

Kang sat in the chair right next to Xiaolian.

"Hi, Xiaolian. Do you remember me?"

"Yes," she said. "You visited me in the hospital."

"And you're talking again. That's great. What do you think of Po Po's cooking?"

"It's delicious."

I set a cup of coffee down in front of Kang. "Hot and black."

"Just how you like your women," Ryan finished.

"Ryan!" I blurted as I did my best to counter my giggles.

"What?" he asked with a shrug. "I thought we were doing the innuendo thing."

"When did we ever do that? And how do you know that word anyway?"

"I hear and see stuff."

"Well, there will be no 'innuendo thing' at the dining table."

"Have you talked with CPS?" Kang asked, quickly changing the subject. "Today's day two with her, right?"

"I haven't. But yes, I think it's a good idea to extend that agreement." I glanced over at Xiaolian. It didn't appear that she knew we were talking about her. "I'll call once we're in the car."

After breakfast, we said our goodbyes to Xiaolian and Po Po and gave the kids a ride to school.

"So what does Xiaolian do all day?" Kang asked after we dropped the kids off.

"She watches a lot of TV with Po Po. The other day, Po Po's friends came over to play mahjong, and Xiaolian joined them. I think she's doing fine. Plus, Lucy always comes straight home from school."

"Seems like she's easily fitting in. You worried at all about the eventual separation?"

"I am."

I dialed the number on the business card Rosales had given me. "Hi, Christine. This is Agent Kane calling. I'm fine, thank you. She's doing well. She's really opened up over the last day, and what she's told me has helped tremendously with our investigation. I'd like to keep her for a bit longer if it's possible. I see. Yes, of course. That was my next question. Uh, huh. Absolutely. It's understandable. Thank you."

Kang glanced my way. "What'd she say?"

"She said there may be separation anxiety, but to mitigate it, I should continue to remind her that we're looking to reunite her with her family."

"Makes sense, unless her family is a bunch of psychos." Kang peered in the rearview mirror before switching lanes.

"Now that we know someone most likely abducted her, I doubt that. They're probably worried to death. I'm sure they have no idea where she is or whether she's alive."

"You said the ship arrived from Taiwan, right? We should share Xiaolian's picture with the Taiwanese police. If she's from there, the parents might have already filed a missing-persons report."

"Good idea." I said. "I'll have Hansen reach out to the right people."

"Your conversation last night..." he prompted.

"Yes, right."

I filled Kang in on everything Xiaolian had told me. "She confirmed a lot of what Medina had already told us, except from her point of view. She never got a good look at any of them or the surrounding area. The only new information she added was that the ship stopped in Honolulu for a refresh of supplies. She said two men brought them more water and food. They also emptied the toilets."

"I don't know why I'm surprised to hear they had working bathrooms in the container. They *were* in there for weeks. You know, I'm actually looking forward to learning more about this container after the CSI team finishes their sweep. Seems like it's equipped to do so much more than what we saw the other day."

"The second thing she mentioned was that one of the men compared each girl with information on a checklist of some sort. Xiaolian was pulled aside from the others."

"Oh, that's interesting."

"Even more I'm thinking this organization, the one responsible for that container, may be nothing more than a smuggling operation catering to different clientele."

"Okay, so Xiaolian was meant for another client, and that client wanted her so he or she could drop her off outside our offices."

"That would be the line of thinking. Stupid I know, but," I shrugged, "I can't imagine what the reasoning is behind that decision. Oh, I almost forgot. One of the men had a tattoo. The only detail she could provide was that it looked like a dragon on a tea cup."

"Millions of dragon tattoos out there."

"Yeah, I know, needle in a haystack, but maybe fate will favor. This dragon guy could be a local."

"While I was with SFPD, we documented the tattoos of

Triad gang members. I'll reach out and get us access. Maybe Xiaolian will recognize it if she saw it again."

"That reminds me, during my last visit to Hong Kong, I learned that HKP documented the tattoos of Triad gang members. It's an extensive collection."

"You still have connections there, right?"

"I do but..."

"What?"

"Does this sound like the Triads to you?"

"My gut says it doesn't fit. It's not how they operate. A lot of thought went into building that container. Costly R&D." Kang rubbed two fingers against his thumb. "Was Xiaolian able to confirm how many girls were in the container?"

"Eleven plus her makes twelve. The exact number of beds in the container."

"Whoever is behind this spent a significant amount of time crunching the numbers. I wonder if twelve bodies is the sweet spot that maximizes profit."

"Also, why limit it to young girls?" I said. "They could ship men, women, whomever. Doesn't matter."

"They could even ship young girls back," Kang added. "The shortage of women in some parts of China have led men with money to pay traffickers to bring them a girl to marry."

"So the prostitution ring continues to have its people gather girls. When they're ready, the trafficker steps in and transports them from A to B. It's possible."

"I wonder who the men were that unloaded the girls from the container. The shipper or receiver?"

CHAPTER TWENTY-EIGHT

AGENT HOUSE GREETED us with a smile when we arrived at the command center, a warehouse. Portable tables had been set up, and various men and women were working on their laptops. Some I recognized; some I didn't. The container was situated near the rear of the building. Large halogen work lamps lit up the inside, where the lab techs were still busy collecting evidence.

"Abby, Kyle. Good morning."

"Hi, Tracy. I see the techs are still at it."

"They are, but we've learned a lot so far. Walk with me."

We followed behind her.

"First off, this is one tricked-out container," she said, looking back at us.

"Xiaolian talked a little about it," I said. "Seemed to have a bunch of creature comforts."

"I'll say. It has a state-of-the-art climate control system, a self-cleaning bathroom, an air infiltration system, and its own power source, run partly by a generator and camouflaged solar panels on the top of the container."

"Solar?" Kang repeated.

"We were just as surprised to find that out as well. They've been removed; the rectangular panels are over there." She pointed at what first glance looked like metal plates painted the same color as the container, but upon closer inspection, I could see the solar cells. They were small and confined to the center of each panel.

"The solar panels recharged the battery-powered generator during the day so it could run all night."

We stopped at the entrance to the container.

"It has an elaborate lighting system controlled by a timer—on during the day, off at night. Not only that, it's completely soundproof." House knocked on the side of the container. "You can't hear a thing that's happening inside from the outside or vice versa."

She led us around to the entrance. "The techs said the entire container is swarming with DNA. We might get lucky, but I'm not holding my breath. I imagine these girls were recruited from rural areas with the promise of easy money. I highly doubt they will have criminal records, but our shippers might have been sloppy and left something behind."

We walked back to the tables. At the front stood a large corkboard noting everything we had learned so far about our investigation. Pinned to it were pictures of Xiaolian, Watts, Medina, and the shipping container. In addition there was a map showing the route the freighter had traveled. There were also screen grabs of the man who had dropped Xiaolian off at the FBI offices, including one of a van.

"That's new," I said, pointing to the vehicle.

"Hansen and Pratt found it when they canvassed the surrounding area for cameras owned by local businesses. It's a black van, so it fits the description. The shot's not the best, but we were able to pull a partial number on the license plate. So far nothing's come of it."

There were also four pieces of paper with blank faces drawn on them and question marks, representing the crew who had unloaded the girls from the container. Identifying them was job one. There was also a sheet of paper representing the other missing girls.

I called Hansen and Pratt over and then updated everyone on my latest conversation with Xiaolian.

"A supply refresh in Honolulu... makes sense," Hansen said.

"I want you and Pratt to get on the phone with the agents in that field office and see if they can locate these individuals," I said.

"Got it," he said, and they hurried away.

Kang pinned two more sheets to the board, representing those individuals.

"Your theory that the traffickers might be someone other than the four individuals who picked up the girls is interesting. If it's true, then there are more moving parts in this puzzle," House said.

"Actually the four individuals who picked up the girls from the container could be the shipper or the receiver, or both. Kang and I just don't think the typical players, like the Triads, are involved. And the Mexican cartels get their girls from Mexico and Central America."

"So the traffickers could just be another small organization entering the trade."

"Yes, but they're smart. What they've set up goes above and beyond what we've seen."

I picked up a pen, scribbled "doctor" on a piece of paper,

and then pinned it to the board. "Xiaolian keeps talking about a doctor or someone who is dressed like one. I have no idea what the connection is, but we should check with the surrounding psychiatric hospitals."

"Has she mentioned anything about her family?" House asked.

"She hasn't, but to be honest, my questioning has always been related to the investigation."

"It seems strange that what she's remembering has only to do with her abduction."

"You're right. I'll try and dig a bit more in that area."

"How much longer are you planning on keeping her?"

"As long as I feel I need to. Each time we talk, her memory becomes clearer. Right now, she's driving this investigation."

Hansen and Pratt returned to the meeting between me, Kang, and House.

"Agent Kane, we have an angle we'd like to pursue," Hansen said. "A lot of these prostitution rings use Craigslist to advertise their girls. The girls who were taken from the container might still be working in the city. We can set up appointments with the providers on the board and try to find out if any of them are part of the container group."

"That's a good idea. Run with it."

After we adjourned our meeting, Kang and I walked over to a table with two large thermal canisters on top of it. One was labeled as coffee, the other as hot water. I removed my tin of tea leaves and proceeded to fix myself a cup while Kang filled a paper cup with the black brew. We took a seat at a nearby table, and I stared off into the distance as I sipped.

"What are you thinking?" Kang asked.

"That I should be back home talking to Xiaolian. That's where my efforts need to be focused."

"I agree. I'll drive you back."

"What will you do?" I asked.

"I'll follow up on that tattoo. See if it leads anywhere."

We sat for a few more minutes, warming our hands with our beverages until my cell phone chimed.

"It's a text from the lab," I said. "They recovered two DNA profiles from the suitcase. One belongs to a Darren Chow."

CHAPTER TWENTY-NINE

DARREN CHOW SAT cross-legged on the small, black leather couch while tapping on the tablet he had cradled in his lap. He was busy juggling a messaging app and an online poker game. Occasionally he took a sip of the milk bubble tea leaning against his thigh.

Sitting next to him was Clifton Wong, but everyone who knew him called him Sticks, not because he was tall and thin—he was actually on the portly side—but because he used chopsticks to eat everything, from French fries, to tacos, to even cereal in the morning. He kept a custom pair on him at all times—even had a special case for them. Sticks was Chow's closest friend. The two had known each other since grade school.

"Yeah!" Chow shouted. "Royal Flush. Cha-ching!" He turned his tablet toward Sticks, a boastful smile stretched across his face.

"Too bad it's not real."

"It will be someday. This is practice, man. As soon as I'm good enough, I'll be competing in international poker tournaments. I'll dress in black, wear shades and a dope hat with my call name embroidered on the front—The Banker."

"Dude, you need to come up with a better name than that," Sticks said.

"What? I'll be taking everyone's money like a bank. Don't you get it?"

"I get it; it's just literal. You need something cool like the Cross-Eyed Chink. People will hear it and think it's racist, but when a Chinese guy shows up they'll be like, 'Oh okay, everything is cool.' Just don't forget to cross your eyes when you play."

"No, it should be associated with his real name," said another young man sitting at a glass-top executive desk. "Something like Chow Wow." He laughed.

"Wait, I got it," a young woman also sitting at the desk chimed in. "Instead of a call name, how about a call slogan—Go home and cook rice! It's like telling the other guys they're done, might as well go home and help with dinner."

The two sitting at the desk, Albert Lim and Angie Dickson, made up the rest of the crew of four. They'd met while attending Stanford University. Chow dropped out after two years, followed by Sticks a few months later.

Lim and Dickson were still enrolled for the time being but had decided to take a semester off and move to the city. They were a couple and had found a small apartment near Golden Gate Park, in a neighborhood called the Panhandle.

The four had been holed up in the small apartment all day, working diligently on their first group venture. About a year and a half ago, they launched their shipping operation. A few days ago, they received their third shipment. There were still kinks that needed to be worked out, but overall they were happy with the results thus far.

Chow was the brain of the operation. He'd had an idea to provide a service to organized crime. Sticks thought he was crazy. Chow of course knew he couldn't do it without him on board.

Sticks was a wizard mathematician with an IQ well over 140. Chow was smart, but nothing like his friend. For as long as he could remember, people had been telling Sticks he had the potential to be amazing in fields ranging from medicine to robotics to space exploration. Sticks, however, had zero interest in pursuing any of those paths. And the more the adult authority figures tried to push that idea on him, the more he rejected it.

Chow understood Sticks though. He knew he didn't ask to be crazy smart. And just because he was, it didn't mean he had to become the poster child for math.

He also knew Sticks hated being told what to do, which Chow often used to his advantage. The best way to convince his friend to go along with his ideas was to tell him it wasn't something he would be interested in or even was capable of doing.

So when Chow bounced the shipping idea off of Sticks, he made sure to present it just so. "Man, it's crazy, but I think it could work. The problem is figuring out whether it's feasible. That alone is a business in itself, something you would job out to Anderson Consulting."

"I don't know. Doesn't sound that difficult to me," Sticks had told him.

"This isn't crunching the numbers on some small project. This is huge. It's international." Then Chow did the move that always worked. He waved off any suggestion that Sticks could do it himself.

A month later, Sticks had crunched the numbers and

figured out every logistic needed in order to traffic a human being on a cargo ship from China to the US. He had accounted for every penny that would be spent and earned. He had tons of spreadsheets and graphs, but Chow never bothered to look at any of it. All he needed to hear from Sticks was that it could be done and they could make a lot of money doing it.

Lim's connection to the business venture was that his family owned a small import/export business, so he brought that expertise to the group. He helped Sticks with the logistics of international shipping and how it worked. His knowledge of the ins and outs of customs, both in China and the US, helped tremendously.

Dickson had a large extended family in Taiwan. She visited them often while growing up. Sometimes she spent entire summers there. While visiting as a teenager, she met a lot of people in the party scene, including her boyfriend at the time. He was older than she and dabbled in the escort business: he paired girls at the local universities with rich businessmen. Dickson watched, learned, and eventually helped out. She felt confident she could find a willing supply of girls.

The Brain.

The Accountant.

The Shipper.

The Madam.

They were the members of the operation they had named Oyster. It wasn't an acronym or code for what they did. They simply loved slurping raw oysters.

Until they could get the business up and running and have all bugs worked out, they had to support the business themselves. Between maxing out their credit cards, making various trips to Vegas where Sticks could count cards, and holding small poker parties in apartments near the Stanford campus, they were able to raise just over one hundred thousand dollars in six months.

But they needed to make their money back quickly.

To do that, they decided early on they would pimp the girls they brought over themselves. And that was exactly what they were doing from that tiny apartment.

Chow had secured the entire floor of the apartment building for one month. There were ten apartments available to him. These were where the girls worked and lived. Oyster kept 70% and the girls got 30% of the fee charged to customers. After thirty days, the girls were returned to Taiwan.

The first shipment of girls netted Oyster about eighty thousand dollars. The second shipment netted them nearly one hundred thousand—Sticks had increased the efficiency of their operation.

From that point forward, they focused on building up their cash reserves so they could eventually expand their operation to multiple containers. Only when they had that in place would they initiate the next step in their business plan: approach local prostitution rings with the idea of using Oyster for their trafficking needs.

Until then, the group agreed that everyone would take a small cut, enough to pay the bills and eat. The rest was to be reinvested back into Oyster.

The way Chow saw things, human trafficking didn't have to be a seedy and dangerous cost of doing business. It could be safe, reliable, and profitable.

CHAPTER THIRTY

KANG and I drove to Chow's last known address. A tactical team had been deployed and would meet us there. We had no idea whether this was a personal address or literally the head-quarters of a smuggling ring. We needed backup.

Chow's apartment was located in an old rattrap building near the corner of Larkin and Austin Street, an area north of the Tenderloin. Not a great area but not crappy either. A lot of neighborhoods in SF mixed that way.

On the way over there, I read a report on my phone that Hansen had pulled on Chow. "Says here he was arrested at age sixteen in Chinatown."

"I thought that name sounded familiar," Kang said. "I was investigating a homicide in Chinatown when we unearthed a fairly large gambling operation. This was about five or six years ago. Anyway, a teenager was caught up in the bust, name was Chow. He essentially was the gang's lookout, nothing major. I remember talking with him. Quiet kid, but well spoken. Didn't come across as the type to get involved with the Triads."

"Could be the same person, but there are a lot of Chows. Did he have a dragon tattoo?"

"Not that I recall."

"Says here he did two years at Stanford University. A dropout. Still sound like your guy?"

"Maybe. Is there a photo?"

"There's a booking photo." I angled my phone so Kang could see Chow's picture.

"That's him. What a shame. I always thought if he stayed out of trouble he'd make something of himself."

"He did. He became a criminal."

The tactical unit reached the location before we did. The commander in charge briefed us as Kang and I put on our bulletproof vests.

"I've got a team stationed at the bottom of the external fire escape," he said. "Other than the front entrance to the building, there's no way out if he decides to run."

We took the stairs up to the fifth floor. The tactical team led the way. Kang and I brought up the rear. On the third floor, an elderly man wearing chinos and a white polo shirt appeared behind us.

"Please don't shoot up the place," he said. "We're short-funded as it is, and there are a ton of repairs needed."

"Sir, I need you to return to your apartment right now."

"I'm the manager here." He held out his hand toward me. "Take it. It's the master key to all the apartments. Please don't kick down the door."

I took the key from him and then told him again to go back to his apartment, which he did, albeit reluctantly.

The team stacked up outside Chow's place. I had the men

pass the key up to the point man. He looked back at me, and I made a turning motion with my hand.

Two minutes later, we were all standing in an empty apartment. No sign of Chow.

"Well, this isn't what we had hoped for," I said.

"Sometimes you win; sometimes you lose," the commander said. "We'll be downstairs if you need us."

He and his team exited the apartment while Kang and I poked around.

Kang came out of the bedroom and returned to the living room, where I was. He shook his head, indicating there was nothing worth noting in the bedroom. "He lives here, but it doesn't seem like he spends much time at the apartment."

"Other than condiments, the refrigerator is empty." I added. "Also the toothpaste in the bathroom looks like it hasn't been touched in a while."

The furniture appeared new, probably all purchased from Ikea. I'd half expected to find mismatched furniture and takeout containers littering the place. There were none. Even the kitchen sink and counters were clear of dishes.

Nothing overtly told us the apartment actually belonged to Chow—no pictures, no personal items that could identify him.

"You think this is even his place?" I asked.

"We should ask the building manager."

"Ask me what?"

We both turned around to find the man standing in the doorway behind us. He began examining the door for damage.

"I'm Agent Kane. This is Agent Kang. We're with the FBI."

"FBI? What are you guys doing here? I'm the manager, and I have the right to know."

"Your name?"

"Swanson. Ed Swanson."

"Mr. Swanson, can you confirm that a man by the name of Darren Chow lives here?"

"He does."

"When did you last see him?"

"Been a while. Maybe a couple of weeks ago, but I don't make it a point to keep an eye on everyone who comes and goes. I'm not that type of manager, you know."

"How well do you know Mr. Chow?"

He shrugged. "I interact with him from time to time."

"Does he live alone? Any girlfriends or friends come around?"

"I never saw anyone with him. Just keeps to himself."

"Did he give you any trouble?" Kang asked.

"He's a decent tenant. Always pays his rent on time. In fact, he's paid up three months in advance."

"Does he own a vehicle, or have you seen him driving one?" I asked.

"I haven't. Plus there's only street parking here, so he could have one and I just never saw it."

I showed Swanson the booking photo I had on my phone. "Is this Mr. Chow?"

He leaned in for a better look. "Yeah, that's him, but he looks a bit younger in the picture."

"He was sixteen at the time," Kang said. "Is there a big change in his appearance?"

Swanson shook his head. "Looks mostly the same. Did something happen to him?"

"We're not at liberty to discuss the details of an ongoing investigation," I answered.

"Investigation? Did he do something wrong? You need to

tell me. I've got a responsibility to keep the building safe for the other residents."

I handed the manager my card. "Call me if you see him."

He took the card and shoved it into the front pocket of his pants. "Well, should I at least tell the guy the FBI is looking for him?"

"For your safety, don't engage. Just call."

Kang and I headed back downstairs. The tactical team was still outside the building. I thanked them for the assistance and cut them loose.

"Who pays their rent up to three months in advance and then barely sticks around?" Kang said as we crossed the street toward his vehicle.

"Yeah, seems strange."

"I wonder…" Kang slipped off his vest. "Maybe the suitcase is his, but he has no involvement in what happened."

"Like someone borrowed it from him?"

"Or maybe he tossed it in the trash and someone scavenged it, or he could have even sold it."

I considered what Kang had said. It was completely plausible.

"We should see if Medina, Watts, or Xiaolian recognizes him," Kang said.

CHAPTER THIRTY-ONE

BACK AT OYSTER HEADQUARTERS, Lim and Dickson were busy engaging with customers. Lim answered the emails from Craigslist. Dickson followed up on the phone to finalize the meet.

"Today's turning out to be a good day," she said. "So far, every girl has cleared at least four clients, and we still got the night, our rush hour."

"Maybe we should jack up the price from three hundred dollars an hour to three fifty," Lim said. "We can still give the girls the same cut and just keep the additional fifty."

"Our strategy with these girls is quantity," Chow said. "If we keep raising the price, the average Joe will go elsewhere to get laid."

"I don't know, man. SF is a tech town. There's a lot of money to throw around," Lim said.

"He's got a point," Sticks added.

"Okay, let's do some split testing," Chow said. "Raise the price on our five most popular girls. If their numbers drop, we'll reduce the price. If not, we'll keep raising it in fifty-dollar increments until we find the sweet spot. Oh, and let's not get too greedy. We'll give those girls their fair share of the price increase."

"If it works, we'll be able to put those other containers into operation sooner," Sticks said.

"Why don't we just keep pimping the girls for a while and make tons of money?" Lim said. "We're learning that side of the business anyway, right? I mean, we'll stick to our original plan of building a shipping business, perfecting it, and then selling it. But if we keep the girls to ourselves, we can double our money. Ain't that right, Sticks?"

Sticks nodded. "Sure, it'll allow us an early exit."

Oyster's initial plan had been to build the trafficking business and stockpile a bunch of cash for a legitimate, yet-to-be-determined start-up. Once those goals were accomplished, they would sell the operation to the highest bidder. None of the four were interested in becoming career criminals.

"I for one would be happier the sooner we're out of this racket," Lim said.

"What's got you so spooked today?" Chow asked.

"I'm not spooked; it's just that the longer we're in this game, the greater the chance we'll get popped. Don't get me wrong... I think we've thought everything through well enough, but we can't really anticipate the unknown. Those guys we hired at the docks. They're the 'unknown' I'm talking about. They could drop the ball for us."

"He's right," Sticks said. "It's simple math. At some point in time, those guys will fuck up."

"And then there's the girl we let go," Lim continued. "That totally deviated from our plans. I know we got paid way above our asking price, but we have no control over what happens to her. At least we can control the girls we have with us. Let's face it. We're book smart not gangster smart. We don't know all the tricks of evading law enforcement."

"I hear you," Chow said. "But if our goal is to be a shipping company, we won't question what the girls are used for, and who is sending or receiving them anyway. Our job will be strictly transport. The only reason we're pimping now is because we're still beta-testing our operation. We'll never have complete control, especially once we start transporting for our customers."

Even with that said, Chow had felt a little uncomfortable with the instructions the customer had given for the girl, but he squashed whatever reservations he had with the belief that their customers would eventually have all sorts of shipping requests.

"Angie, what are your thoughts?" Chow asked.

"The sooner we get those other containers into operation, the sooner we meet our capital goal and can walk away. I like risk but good risk. And Albert's right—we lack the experience that comes with years of being a criminal."

"Okay, here's what we do. We'll only guarantee safe delivery from port to port. The customer is responsible for drop-off and pick-up. If we feel we can expand our services beyond that at a later date, then we'll do that. How does that sound?"

Everyone nodded.

Lim looked at his watch. "It's past lunchtime. I'll ask the girls what they're craving."

CHAPTER THIRTY-TWO

WITH CHOW ADDED to the equation, Kang and I decided to sit on his apartment for a little bit. His DNA was found on the suitcase, and we needed to rule out whether he was involved. Kang sent the photo we had of Chow to Agent House and asked her to pass the picture on to Customs so they could be on the lookout for him. Also, they currently had Medina and Watts in custody and could show the photo to both of them.

"What about Xiaolian? We can swing by your house and then circle back here after?"

I glanced at my watch. We were only a ten-minute drive away. I thought about just texting the picture to Po Po and asking her to show it to Xiaolian but reconsidered when I looked at the picture again. I didn't want to send Po Po a mug shot.

"Let's take a ride there."

When we got there, Po Po was preparing lunch: egg drop soup with won ton. Of course once Kang and I got a sniff, we decided we could spare a bit more time and slurp soup.

Xiaolian was on the third floor watching TV in the entertainment room. Since the soup needed ten more minutes on the stove, I went up there to talk to her.

"Hi, Xiaolian. What are you watching?"

"I don't know the name of this show, but these people have so many things."

It was a show about people who hoard items. I switched off the television and took a seat next to her on the couch. "I want to show you a picture." I held out my phone. "Do you recognize this man?"

She looked at Chow's photo briefly before shaking her head. "No. Who is he?"

"We think he's one of the men who took you out of the container. Take a closer look."

She stared at the picture.

"Nothing looks familiar? His nose or chin?" I pressed.

"I don't know."

"Okay. I think lunch is ready. Let's go downstairs."

We ate quickly and didn't dilly-dally, as we were keen on returning to Chow's apartment. I would have asked Hansen and Pratt to sit on the apartment, but they were busy pursuing the Craigslist angle, which I thought could be extremely helpful.

On the drive back to Chow's place, House called, and I put her on speakerphone.

"Neither Medina nor Watts recognizes Chow," she said.

"You think they're covering?"

"I don't think so. The best I got was a 'maybe' from Medina. Even though he saw all four individuals, he said he always made sure to avoid looking directly at any of them. Watts only spoke with the driver of the van, and he simply gave me a shrug. Any luck with Xiaolian?"

"No."

"So where does that leave us with Chow?" House asked.

"Unless we can place him at the port, nowhere," I said. "Nothing at his apartment suggested he's involved. It might be a different story if we question him. We're sitting on his apartment for a bit to see if he turns up."

Kang parked across the street from Chow's apartment.

"I'm getting a coffee. You want some hot water?"

"Please."

While Kang went on a beverage run, I removed a pen and small notebook from my purse and started making a list of what we knew so far, to keep my thinking straight.

- *Xiaolian and eleven girls were trafficked from Taiwan to the US via a cargo ship.*
- *The ship stopped in Honolulu. Two men refreshed supplies.*
- *Corey Watts allowed two black vans with three men and one woman to enter the port.*
- *Carlos Medina moved the container to a remote location inside the port.*
- *Three men and one woman unloaded the girls from the container and into two vans.*
- *One of those individuals might be Darren Chow. One of them has a dragon tattoo.*
- *Xiaolian was singled out from the group.*
- *She was stuffed in a suitcase and left outside the FBI offices.*
- *The whereabouts of the four individuals and the girls they took are unknown.*
- *Xiaolian's memory is limited to the container and the four individuals. She remembers nothing about her*

family or home or anything personal with the
exception of a "doctor."

The click of the door handle jolted me out of my thought process. Kang opened the door and passed me my cup of hot water before taking his seat.

"Anything exciting happen while I was gone?" he asked as he shifted to a comfortable position.

"Nah, I was just thinking about what we know so far."

"And?"

"It's not much."

I handed Kang my notes and then dug into my purse for my tin of tea leaves. Two pinches into the cup before sealing the lid back on.

Kang nodded as he read what I wrote. "Looks dismal."

He handed me back my notebook and then removed his cell phone from his pocket. "SFPD emailed me the file of Triad tattoos they have. Maybe we'll have some luck there." He scrolled through pictures while slurping his coffee.

"Anything?"

"None of them seem to match the description that Xiaolian gave you. You think she might have remembered wrong?"

"It's a possibility. You said there were eight dragon tattoos on file?"

"Yeah."

"Email them to me. I'll show them to her later."

"How extensive is HKP's collection of tattoos?" Kang asked.

"It's pretty big, but it's categorized. A keyword search for dragon and teacup is all that's needed. I should receive what they have sometime tonight."

We sat there for a solid three hours before my stomach

grumbled. I remembered being a newbie on stakeouts. I didn't mind doing them. The anticipation that something exciting could happen, like a foot chase, kept me focused. That thrill had slowly disappeared over the years.

I was about to ask Kang if he wanted to get something to eat when my phone rang. It was Hansen.

"I'm with Kang," I said. "I'm putting you on speakerphone."

"So we had a promising breakthrough with our search. We've located a building that appears to house a number of Asian girls. Pratt and I made appointments with different girls from Craigslist, and they were both from the same location. Plus we both spoke to the same girl to confirm the appointments. It's obvious the same person is managing both of them."

"Were they Chinese?" Kang asked.

"I think so."

"You mean you can't tell the difference between a Chinese girl, a Japanese girl, and a Korean girl?" Kang asked.

There was silence on the other end as Kang and I muffled our laughter.

"I'm kidding," he said. "Go on."

Hansen let out a nervous laugh. "Uh, okay. Neither girl could speak any English. And the apartments were small studios, just a bed and bathroom. Nothing else."

"No sign of a man?" I asked.

"I passed a young Asian man in the hall on my way to the elevator. He had exited an apartment, and he was heading toward the apartment I had just come from. I tried to slow down to see if he would go in, but he eyed me until I got in the elevator. He didn't look like Darren Chow."

"You didn't happen to notice if he had a dragon/teacup tattoo on his arm?"

"The hall was dimly lit, and we passed each other fairly fast. With that said, we think it's worth hitting the place. Two of the eleven apartments were housing the girls."

Just then Pratt came on the line "Hey, this is Pratt speaking. I also heard moaning from another apartment on the way out, which makes three apartments servicing men. We're willing to bet every apartment on the floor is doing the same thing. Worst-case scenario, we break up a prostitution ring."

"I agree. Let's rally the troops and figure out a plan of attack."

CHAPTER THIRTY-THREE

IT WAS a little after five in the afternoon. The tactical team, Kang, Hansen, Pratt, and I had been conducting surveillance on the building for roughly two hours. During the course of that time, we noted twelve different men entering the building and staying inside anywhere from twenty minutes to an hour. The last one was out in ten.

"Speedy he is," Pratt said over the comms in a Yoda-like voice.

We saw enough to confirm what Hansen and Pratt suspected that I gave the tactical unit the go-ahead to move into place. Once SFPD secured a perimeter around the building, we entered and made our way up the stairwell.

Two men were assigned to each apartment. On the commander's go, the teams breached the doors at the same time.

"FBI! Open up!" The phrase echoed repeatedly, followed by battering rams smashing into doors.

After the commotion died down, we surveyed our catch: eleven Chinese girls who all looked eighteen or under, two customers, and four other individuals, one who looked extremely familiar to me.

I walked up to that person. "I've been looking for you."

He wore a gray hoodie. I pushed up both sleeves to reveal a tattoo on his right forearm: a dragon coiled around a teacup.

We took everyone into custody and then transferred the group to the holding center at our offices. According to the IDs we collected, the little prostitution gang was made up of Darren Chow, Albert Lim, Angie Dickson, and Clifton Wong.

I entered the room where Chow was being held. His hands were in cuffs and resting on the table in front of him. I sat down opposite him.

"I'm Agent Kane. I already know you're Darren Chow."

I opened the file folder I had brought with me. "Let's see... charged with illegal gaming at age sixteen and received misdemeanor probation." I glanced briefly at him. "I suppose you were only working for the mahjong parlor and nothing more. Maybe saw it as an easy way to put some extra cash into your pockets."

Chow looked away from me and stared at the wall.

"It also says here you attended Stanford University. One would think that you turned your life around and were making a productive go of it. But after two years you left, and now you're facing a whole slew of federal charges that include trafficking of a minor, kidnapping of a minor, forced prostitution of a minor, conspiracy to accept money to smuggle a minor into the United States... The list goes on."

I closed the folder. Chow still wouldn't look at me.

"It's clear to us that you and your gang are prostituting these girls, but we also know you're responsible for smuggling them into the country. We have your high-tech shipping container.

Did you know that, or were you under the impression it was on a boat heading back to Taiwan? Pretty impressive, I must say. Everyone around here took a look."

Still Chow said nothing.

"We know Carlos Medina, a forklift operator at the port, works for you. He moves your container to an area where you can safely unload your human cargo. We also know Corey Watts, a port security guard, allows you access to the grounds. And now we know all about your prostitution ring involving illegally smuggled minors. Anything you want to say? No? Nothing? Okay I'll continue. Thanks to that tattoo you have on your arm, we have someone who identified you as the person who took her out of the container and later gave her an injection of propofol. And lastly, which is the capper to all of this, we recovered your DNA from a suitcase that was stuffed with a living girl and left outside of our offices. If you want, we can show you the video footage for refresher."

Chow finally shifted his gaze to me. "Lawyer."

I smiled. "You can have your lawyer, but it won't help. You see, right now, my colleagues are talking to your friends. I'm pretty sure they're spilling their guts and pointing the finger at you in hopes of maximizing their deals. I would offer you a deal, but I really don't see what you could offer us in return. Honestly, I have no idea why I'm even talking to you. You're so screwed."

A smile formed on Chow's face; actually, it was more like a smug smirk.

"You have no idea how wrong you have it, Agent Kane."

CHAPTER THIRTY-FOUR

I EXITED the room that held Chow. Kang was next door questioning one of the other individuals running the operation. Hansen and Pratt had each taken one as well. I was about to check on the young ones when Kang appeared.

"What's the story?" he asked.

"He's not talking. Wants a lawyer."

"He knows he's screwed."

"Pretty much. I laid it out neatly for him. What about your guy?"

"His name is Clifton Wong, a.k.a. Sticks. Apparently he's been a friend of Chow since they were knee high. Both attended Stanford and dropped out around the same time. He's starting to talk. So far he's admitted that he's the money guy, does all the accounting/cost control stuff. Might be a good idea to play Chow off of him, considering their relationship."

We entered the room together. Sticks sat at the table, with his head down and legs bouncing relentlessly.

"Hello, Sticks. I'm Agent Kane."

"Uh, hello."

"That's an interesting nickname."

"I like chopsticks."

"I see. Well, Agent Kang tells me you attended Stanford University."

"Yeah, for two years."

"You didn't finish?"

He shook his head. "I got bored."

"I see. So you were eager to get out into the world and make your mark rather than sit cooped up in a classroom."

"Um, I guess you could say that."

"And heading up an international human trafficking conglomerate was your idea of contributing to society."

"Wait, what do you mean? I didn't head anything up."

"You're the brains, right? Everyone knows the money guy is the smartest and the one who really runs an operation. So..."

"I'm not the one in charge, I mean, yeah, I'm the money guy, if that's what you want to call it, but—"

"Your friend next door, Darren, says you're the one who dreamed all of this up. You were the one who figured out how to make everything work. The container... you singlehandedly put that together. Not in the physical sense, but you know what I mean."

"No, that's not true."

"You didn't cost out everything?"

"I did, but—"

"Well, that means you have to know the intimate details of everything. Who else would have that knowledge but the guy who thought it up in the first place?"

"You've got it all wrong."

"So you're not involved? You just happened to swing by to visit your buddy at the wrong time? Is that what you're saying?"

"Whatever." Sticks waved off my accusation. "I'm not hearing any of that."

"Well, you better because with all the federal charges stacked against you, life in prison with no chance for parole is exactly what you'll get. We're handing the attorney general a slam-dunk case. And he loves putting away the heads of criminal organizations."

"I'm not the head. Darren needed someone to figure out the costs for this operation, so I did exactly what he wanted."

"Wait. Are you telling us that he's the real mastermind behind all of this?"

"It's his idea. He got the rest of us involved."

"Why should we believe you? Haven't you two been best friends since you were kids?"

Sticks let out a breath as he shook his head. "This is all screwed up. It wasn't supposed to happen this way."

"Why don't you tell us exactly how it should have happened?"

"If I do, what do I get in return? I don't want to go to jail."

"That's a tall request. We know so much already and have the evidence to prove it." I turned to Kang. "What do you think?"

He shrugged and then buried his hands in the front pockets of his slacks. "I guess if he tells us everything, that's gotta count for something."

"Yeah, it should," Sticks added.

Sticks went on to tell us how Chow approached him with the idea of developing a trafficking business.

"He said gangs that needed prostitutes could get them easily outside of the US but faced the hassle of bringing them into the country. They also didn't put much thought into it either. The result is unhealthy girls and unreliability. He figured if we could nail the transport, we could then service these people."

"But you guys were also prostituting those girls back at the building," I said.

"It was temporary. We needed to make our money back, plus we wanted to understand their aspect of the business. Once we paid off our debt and built up a cash cushion, we planned to stop and just focus on transporting. The end game was to always sell the operation off to the highest bidder and walk away and start up a legitimate business. And those girls aren't being forced. They were recruited. They stay here for a month, make a bunch of money, and then we ship them back. They signed up for it. We would never force someone."

"But you were eventually willing to transport girls who might have been kidnapped and forced into prostitution, isn't that right?"

Sticks said nothing and looked away briefly. "Our goal was to deliver healthy girls on a reliable schedule. We can't vet every girl who is brought to us. It's like FedEx can't be expected to look inside every package they ship, right?"

"They're not shipping human beings illegally into this country." I shook my head, pursed my lips for a moment, then said, "I don't know if you've made a strong enough case for us to cut you a deal. What do you think, Agent Kang?"

"I think someone is heading to jail for a long time," Kang said.

"I don't know what else to tell you. You already know everything."

"Who do you guys really work for?" I asked.

"What do you mean? We don't work for anyone. We don't have any customers. I mean, we were pretty much still beta-testing and working out the kinks."

"You and your partners, with the exception of Mr. Chow, don't have criminal records. I find it hard to believe that you four somehow figured this all out with absolutely no experience."

Sticks told us about the others and the specialties they brought to the group. To be honest, I was impressed—even with those backgrounds, what they'd pulled off was incredibly sophisticated. We had never seen a smuggling operation like this. Even Customs and Border Protection was caught off guard. The ability to consider every detail so thoroughly was mind blowing. If it wasn't for Xiaolian being left outside our building, I believed they would have gone unchecked and fulfilled their goals without anyone finding out. Which raised the question: why did they do something so dumb?

"Tell me about the girl in the suitcase."

"What girl in the suitcase?"

"The one you guys left outside our offices."

Sticks crinkled his brow. "Are you talking about the girl who looks like you?"

"So you do know about her?"

"I don't know what you're talking about. I mean, yeah, I can see the resemblance. Are you family or something?"

"That girl was stuffed into a suitcase and left outside this office building in the early morning, the day after your shipment arrived."

"That's impossible. We would never do something like that. It's stupid. It would jeopardize..."

"That's right, your operation. Start talking."

He sighed loudly and stared at the ceiling for a moment. "She was a last-minute addition to the shipment. A customer had approached us... well, approached Darren. He vouched for the person. They were willing to pay triple what he originally asked for to bring the girl to the US."

"Why not just fly her to the States?"

"I dunno. Maybe she has passport problems."

"The other girls have passports?"

"Some do. But that's why I have a checklist with their names and pictures. It's how I know we received what was shipped."

"So your organization didn't arrange the shipment in Taiwan."

"Sort of. Angie flew there about a month ago, recruited the girls, and then left instructions with her ex-boyfriend. He gets everybody on the ship for a fee."

"Angie had nothing to do with the recruitment of this particular girl?"

"No, it was arranged through Darren. Someone we don't know met up with Angie's ex at the ship. And this person sent a picture of the girl to Darren so we could cross-check on our end."

"So that's why you singled her out from the other girls when you unloaded the container?"

"Uh, yeah. Someone was supposed to meet us at the port so we could hand her off and be done with it."

"But..."

"Darren said the plan changed. The person who was supposed to pick up the girl couldn't and—"

"Wait, was it one person or a group?"

"I'm not sure. Anyway, whoever was supposed to pick her up asked that we hold on to her for a few hours, so we did. Later we got another call to drop her off at a meeting point. Darren said he would deal with it."

"He went alone?"

"Yeah, it was late. We were tired."

"And you thought nothing of it?"

"It was late," Sticks said with a raised voice. "We were all tired. No one argued. The next morning when we woke, Darren had already returned. He said everything went as planned. He showed us the payment. Eighteen thousand in cash."

I turned my back to Sticks and looked at Kang with raised eyebrows. He motioned toward the door, and we exited the room.

'Didn't see that coming," Kang said.

I agreed, and then I shared what Chow had told me earlier: that I had it all wrong. "Maybe he really did make a hand-off to another person."

"And that person is really the person who dropped Xiaolian off outside our office building," Kang said.

"We all assumed that they dropped Xiaolian off because they unloaded her from the container, and she identified the tattoo on Chow's arm, and we found his DNA in the suitcase. It's a logical conclusion."

"So maybe delivering her in a suitcase was part of the request."

"Hold that thought."

I poked my head back in the room and asked Sticks if Darren had left for the meeting point with a suitcase.

"I didn't see him leave with one," he answered.

I shut the door.

"Maybe he picked one up on the way or had it stashed in the van," Kang said.

"Well, if he didn't, then we have another party involved."

CHAPTER THIRTY-FIVE

WE MET up with Hansen and Pratt after they finished with their questioning.

"According to Lim and Dickson, they all met while attending Stanford," Hansen said. "These two lovebirds are still enrolled but took a semester off."

All in all, the three who talked told the same story. Chow, on the other hand, remained tight-lipped.

"Abby, maybe it is what it is," Kang said. "We got three of them giving us the exact same story about the operation and Xiaolian. Chow not talking is most likely him trying to cover his butt. He knows he's screwed."

"So someone spends a lot of money to smuggle her into the US only to turn her over to the FBI," I said. "That just makes no sense. Who? Why?"

"Chow's the only one who talked to this mystery person or persons," Kang said. "We need him to talk, which he isn't doing. Unless we cut him a deal, there's no reason for him to say anything."

"How badly do you want to find the person who dropped off Xiaolian?" Hansen asked.

"What are you getting at?"

"Well, the way I see it, we took down what was heading toward a huge trafficking scheme. We got in early and *not* because we were investigating these four. They weren't even on our radar. We stopped a beast in its first few steps. Would you really want to cut a deal to the guy who organized all of this just to find out who dropped the girl off? I mean, she's fine. She's not hurt. She wasn't forced into prostitution. She was just dropped off. Maybe she came from a bad home and someone wanted her out and far from that environment. Far enough to smuggle her into the States and then turn her over to the FBI in hopes we file for asylum status."

Hansen had a good point. "You're right. We did end up catching the big fish. Agent Hansen, Agent Pratt, your hunch about Craigslist paid off. Excellent job."

"We just might make investigators out of you two." Kang chuckled.

I had Hansen and Pratt take the lead on questioning the girls and notifying CPS. Depending on their situation, CPS could lobby to have them stay in the country, but I doubted that would be the case. They apparently came over willingly and had expected to go home after a month or so. Unless something significant arose from questioning them, I expected them to be deported swiftly.

That also meant Xiaolian would be deported. She had entered the country illegally and had no family connection here. With the investigation winding down, there was no need for the FBI to retain her.

I spent the remainder of my time at the office writing up a

report until Lucy called asking if I would be home in time for dinner. "Of course I will. See you soon."

I bade goodbye to Kang and then stuck my head into Reilly's office to let him know I would have a report on his desk the following morning.

"And the girl... are you handing her over to CPS?" he asked, reminding me again we had no need to hold Xiaolian.

I knew deep down Reilly wouldn't support cutting Chow a deal to find out who Xiaolian's handler was. We had scored a big bust for the department, and the investigation could be neatly closed.

If anything, I could question Chow after he spoke with his lawyer to see if he could help with Xiaolian, but even then, what was the point? Eventually she would be deported. Whether she was forced or had come willingly to the US, she'd arrived illegally. Plus Reilly was under the impression we would now be winding down the investigation. Xiaolian was a non-issue for him.

I arrived home to Lucy moaning she was starving and near death. She feigned dizziness and dragged her feet as she walked to the dinner table. "My God, I could never survive a hunger strike," she said.

I asked her why on earth would she face a hunger strike.

"I'm just saying, if I had to, I wouldn't last very long."

"What about you, Xiaolian? Are you starving too?"

"Yes, Po Po's cooking is the best."

Po Po waved her off playfully.

The two seemed to genuinely get along. Whenever I asked Xiaolian what they talked about during the day, she would always shrug and say, "I dunno. A lot of things."

The only people I'd known Po Po to have engaging conversations with were her friends. She talked to Ryan, Lucy, and me, but it was nothing like the nonstop chatter she had with her group. And they always spoke in Chinese, shouting over one another, with a lot of finger pointing and dismissive hand gestures. They seemed happier that way.

After dinner and spending time with Lucy and Ryan, Xiaolian and I retreated to her room for our nightly conversation. Part of me felt I really didn't need to have the talk. It wasn't imperative that we find the person who had abandoned her. And so far, that seemed to be the only thing that had happened, outside of being brought illegally into the country. Even if I did lobby CPS to take her in permanently, they would have to file for a T-1 visa, and even then it wasn't a guarantee she would be issued one.

Why I even had those thoughts were a mystery to me. Xiaolian wasn't family. She wasn't my responsibility. She just looked a lot like me.

She climbed onto her bed, and I sat on the edge of the mattress.

"Today we caught the men who took you out of the container," I said rather bluntly.

"Oh? What will happen to them?"

"They will go to prison. They did a very bad thing."

I didn't think I needed to explain what happened with the other girls, even if they had supposedly volunteered.

"The leader of their group had a dragon tattoo like you described, so you helped us catch them. His name is Darren Chow. Does that sound familiar?"

"No."

"It's okay. I'm just asking. However, there is something I wanted to clarify with you. When you told me about the tattoo, you said you saw it when he injected you. Are you sure about that?"

Xiaolian's crunched her brow. "Yes, I think so. But maybe I saw it when he put me in the van. Now I'm confused. I'm not sure anymore."

"Okay, let's start from the beginning. There's no rush, so let's take our time. After leaving the container, you got inside of a van, right?"

"Yes."

"You may have seen the tattoo then, but you can't quite remember right now?"

"Sorry."

"You're doing fine. Okay, once you're in the van, where did you go? Do you remember?"

She took a deep breath and let it out slowly. "The van stopped, and we waited for a long time before they told us to get out. We went into a building and took the elevator to the top floor, and then they put me in an apartment by myself."

"And the other girls?"

She shrugged.

Probably the building where we busted Chow's organization.

"Then what?"

"I fell asleep. Later one of the men woke me."

"Did you see his face?"

"He had sunglasses and a big coat that covered his head."

"Was it the man with the tattoo?"

"I'm not sure. I don't remember seeing one."

"Okay, so what happened next?"

"We went back to the van."

"Just the two of you?"

She nodded. "I remember it was still dark outside. We drove

around, but I don't know where. He made me lie down in the back. I think I fell asleep again."

"So you think maybe you don't remember him giving you an injection?"

Her eyes shifted from side to side as she sat quietly for a few moments. "No, I remember him giving me a shot. I did fall asleep, but I woke up. He told me he had to give me my medicine. After that, I felt really tired."

"Do you remember getting inside of a suitcase?" I quickly found the picture of the suitcase on my phone and showed it to her.

She took a closer look.

"Take your time."

"I remember."

"What? What do you remember?"

"He put me in the suitcase."

"Are you sure?"

She nodded enthusiastically. "Yes, because that's when I saw the tattoo on his arm."

CHAPTER THIRTY-SIX

THE '77 MONTE CARLO sped north on the Interstate 580. Its golden paint had long ago surrendered to the elements and was now faded and patchy beyond repair. Its hood extended out, like a long snout, sniffing the road ahead. The short trunk helped to enhance it.

In the driver seat, with one arm resting on the top of the steering wheel, the other hanging out the window, a young man stared absentmindedly ahead. His black hair was neatly slicked back, cropped short on the sides. He wore black jeans, leather dress shoes, and a navy-blue designer button-down shirt, the top two buttons undone. A gold chain, rings on every finger, and a bracelet completed his outfit, along with a heavy application of cologne.

Another man sat next to him. He wore a similar outfit but with a black dress shirt and silver chain, rings, and bracelets instead. The cologne was different, but equally heavy.

Their features were the only thing identical about them.

The Chan brothers, Walter and Alonzo, had flown into

Reno from Singapore. They preferred the small town over its larger sister city, Las Vegas.

They'd hailed a taxi at the airport and told the driver to take them to the nearest used-car dealer. There they purchased the Monte Carlo in cash for three thousand dollars. They then drove into town.

Flashing neon signs burned brightly on both sides of the strip, enticing gamblers into the casinos. A welcome arch outfitted with two thousand LED bulbs sparkling around the city's slogan, "The biggest little city in the world," stretched across the street.

They stopped at an all-you-can-eat seafood buffet in one of the hotels. Walter gorged on Alaskan king crab, Alonzo preferred to fill up on raw oysters.

Content. They'd returned to the Monte Carlo and drove until they found a small motel with vacancies. There they waited.

Quietly.

Patiently.

At exactly seven p.m., their contact arrived. A brief conversation took place before the brothers handed over a paper bag filled with cash and received a suitcase in return.

With their business transaction completed, they exited the room, walked to the largest casino in town, and spent the remainder of the night at the Pai Gow tables. They ended their winning streak just before five in the morning and purchased two coffees from a nearby convenience store before heading back to the motel.

Inside the room, Walter opened the suitcase they had received earlier and removed four handguns and four sound suppressors. He handed two of each over to his brother and kept the other pair for himself. He strapped on a double holster and tucked the weapons away. He then slipped on a sport jacket. His brother did exactly the same.

They sipped their coffee quietly, finishing it all before exiting the room and driving away in the Monte Carlo.

Walter drove. Alonzo rode shotgun.

Their destination wasn't far from where they were staying—a ten-minute drive tops—just slightly outside the downtown area.

It was a little before six in the morning and the sun had just cracked the horizon when Walter parked on the quiet street lined with older, ranch-style homes. They slipped quietly out of the vehicle and walked up the short driveway of a light-blue house.

Walter led the way to the side of the structure, through a wooden gate that connected to a concrete wall separating the property from the house next door. The backyard had a pool with decayed leaves littering the bottom, and no outdoor furniture to be seen. The brothers removed their guns and screwed the suppressors on.

The sliding glass door leading into the house hadn't been locked, and they quietly entered the premises. They stood in an open kitchen with an attached dining area. The counters and a small glass-top table were littered with newspapers, old pizza boxes, and Chinese takeout containers. Empty beer cans were scattered across the carpeted floor in the living room. More empty takeout containers sat on the coffee table, along with a tall glass bong.

Walter used his gun to point to the hallway, where the bedrooms were. There were four doors; all of them were shut except for one—a bathroom. Two of the bedroom doors were opposite each other. At the end of the hall was the third one.

Alonzo choose the door on the left, leaving Walter to enter the one on the right. In Alonzo's room, there was a single mattress on the floor. A man with a scruffy beard lay on it, snoring softly under a thin sheet. Alonzo bent down for a better look and compared the man's face to a photo on his cell phone. The man in the bed didn't match the man in the photo. He left the bedroom.

Walter exited his bedroom and shook his head. They both looked at the room at the end of the hall.

Inside the master bedroom was a large bed in the center with the headboard flush against the wall. There was a large dresser made of the same dark wood as the bed frame. It had a large vanity mirror attached to it, but there were no bottles of perfume or cosmetics one would expect to find on such a dresser top.

Walter walked over to one side of the bed, where a large man slept on his side with his potbelly spilling over onto the fitted sheet. His mouth hung slightly open, and he breathed hard. His head was completely shaven—a spider tattoo covered most of it.

Alonzo stood on the other side of the bed, where a blond female slept, her mascara smeared below her eyes. She had frosted locks and large fake breasts. Her pink nipples stood erect. They were long, almost an inch.

Both individuals were partially covered by a chocolate-brown flat sheet. The pillowcases didn't match; they were off-white. At the foot of the bed, scrunched up, was a comforter that did match the sheets.

Walter removed his phone and compared the face of the

man with the photo on the screen. He looked at Alonzo and nodded. He aimed his handgun at the head of the man. Alonzo aimed his at the female.

Walter fired once, and the man's head jerked from the impact, the pillowcase soiled by the red spray. Alonzo didn't pull his trigger. He continued to watch the woman. She hadn't stirred. He holstered his gun, and the two of them exited the house the same way they entered.

From Reno, the drive to San Francisco International Airport would take roughly four hours, maybe a bit longer. Along the way, the brothers stopped in Sacramento for a quick bite at a taco stand. Walter ordered four carnitas tacos, and Alonzo ordered four fish tacos. They both chose horchata for a drink.

While eating, Walter's cell phone rang. He pressed the phone against his ear but said nothing. Alonzo paid no attention and continued to munch on his taco. About a minute later, Walter disconnected the call and pocketed the phone.

"Our plan has changed," he said. "We have another job."

He picked up his taco and continued eating.

CHAPTER THIRTY-SEVEN

When I arrived at the office the next morning, Kang was already at his desk eating a salted bagel sandwich with egg, ham, and cheese flowing out from the sides.

"That looks good," I said.

He mumbled something and then pointed to a bag sitting on my desk.

I smiled at him. "You always think of me. Thank you."

Even though I had eaten a few silver dollars that morning with the kids, I'd never been one to turn down food, even if I was full. It was a knee-jerk reaction that I'd always had. I didn't know why. I had never wanted for food when growing up. My parents provided more than enough, and I ate more than my share. Maybe that was it. Maybe I'd had too much food while growing up.

I dropped my purse at my desk and headed to the breakroom to fix a cup of tea. When I returned, Hansen and Pratt were talking to Kang.

"Good morning, Agent Kane," Hansen said. "We wanted to let you two know how the questioning went last night."

"Anything useful?" I asked as I sat.

"Nothing revealing, mostly confirming what we already knew."

"Any of those girls see or hear anything about the person who dropped Xiaolian off at the ship?" I removed the bagel sandwich from the paper bag. "You guys hungry?" I held out the sandwich.

They shook their heads simultaneously.

"They said Xiaolian was already inside the container asleep in a bed when they arrived," Hansen said. "They didn't know her, so no one really paid any attention to her. I did ask them if they thought it was strange that a girl so young took the trip with them. I got a bunch of shrugs as answers."

"How is it they can spend all that time cooped up in that container and not learn anything about each other?" Kang asked.

"A few of the girls knew each other, so they just hung out together. The rest of the girls kept to themselves. Most had already dabbled briefly in the escort business. They're not as young as they look. They range in age from sixteen to eighteen. We contacted CPS. They want to conduct their own interview with each girl before turning them over to immigration for deportation."

"Did they seem broken up that their money-making scheme was cut short?" Kang asked.

Hansen shook his head as he looked at Pratt, who also shook his head. "Nope. They're too scared, probably thinking their next trip would be to a prison cell," Hansen said.

"Where are we on the two men who provided supplies in Honolulu?" I asked before taking a bite of my sandwich.

"They've been detained. Same deal as Medina and Watts.

They were offered money to do that one thing. They were told nothing else, and they never got a good look at the person who made the arrangements. Someone from Chow's crew probably flew to Honolulu to recruit those men."

Pratt spoke up. "One last thing, the cyber crime unit is combing the gang's laptops and cell phones. Possible we might catch a break with something useful."

"Did Chow's lawyer show up yet?"

"Showed up last night. He's representing all four of them. I did overhear him tell Chow he would expedite his bail hearing so that it took place today."

"That's quick," I said between chews.

"Is something wrong?" Hansen asked.

"No, but now that Chow's talked to his lawyer, I want to see if he is willing to loosen his mouth and tell us what he knows about the customer who had Xiaolian shipped."

"I'll let the lawyer know we want to question Chow again."

After our meeting with Hansen and Pratt, I continued working on my report for Reilly, the first step in winding down the investigation. I was already convinced by then that we wouldn't learn who sent Xiaolian to the US. But I was ninety percent sure it was Chow who'd dropped her off at our offices—that is, if Xiaolian's memory was correct about seeing his tattoo before getting inside the suitcase. There was a chance that Chow had handed her off to someone else, but my gut wasn't buying it.

Later, Hansen let me know that Chow's lawyer agreed to meet at the federal courthouse next door after the bail hearing, which was set for one thirty that afternoon.

A little before noon, Kang bugged me to have lunch with him. It was food-truck day at the Civic Center. Between eight to ten trucks would show, offering everything from Korean tacos to smoked ribs to steak sandwiches to curry empanadas.

"Five minutes and I'll be done," I said.

Kang paced the area near our desks, jingling the change in the front pocket of his pants—his passive way of telling me to hurry up.

"Okay, I just hit send. We're good to go."

"Come on. We gotta hurry before the lines get long."

On the way to the elevator, my cell phone rang. It was Po Po.

"Hi. Is everything okay?"

"Xiaolian disappear!"

CHAPTER THIRTY-EIGHT

KANG and I wasted no time jumping into my car and racing back to the house. I had asked Po Po two questions before disconnecting the call. *Are you safe?* Her answer was yes. *Are the doors locked?* They weren't. I told her to lock herself in and that I was on my way.

With the siren blaring from my Charger, we were making record time. Still I couldn't help but think Po Po was in some immediate danger. It was obvious to me that someone who was connected to Chow had come after Xiaolian. What I couldn't know was whether or not that was all they wanted. Kang called his old precinct in Chinatown and had them send a unit over to my address.

"Done. A patrol car will be there in the next few minutes."

"Will you call her?" I asked Kang as I drove.

He called Po Po, and she picked up. She said everything was fine and not to worry about her.

A patrol car was already at the house when we arrived, and it appeared the situation was under control. Still, I made a beeline inside.

"Po Po!" I called out as I burst through the front door.

She stepped out of the kitchen and into the hallway.

"Thank God you're okay," I said, giving her a hug.

"I tell you before I okay. But I don't know where Xiaolian go."

"Tell me everything, from the beginning."

Kang entered the house just then.

"I prepare lunch for Xiaolian. When I go to call her, she not there."

"Not where? In her room?"

"She in the backyard."

"What was she doing?"

Po Po shrugged. "Fresh air. She go out there many times."

"Oh. Okay, so you went into the backyard and she wasn't there. How long was she alone?"

Po Po thought for a moment. "Maybe she got out about thirty minutes before."

I studied the lock on the door leading to the screened-in porch, careful not to touch it. It seemed to be working and undamaged. Kang and I looked around the porch but saw nothing out of the ordinary.

"Don't touch the knob," I said. "I want to dust for prints."

We exited the house through the front door and walked over to the side, where a path led to the rear of the house. Grass had a hard time growing there because of the lack of direct sunlight, so the ground was soft. We treaded cautiously.

"There," I said, pointing at the ground.

"I see it," Kang said.

There was an imprint of a shoe, and it was too big to be Xiaolian's—evidence I didn't want squandered. I put a call in to the lab and had them send a team out to the house.

When forensics arrived, they dusted the entire porch for prints. They also found another shoe impression that matched the one I'd found. They snapped pictures and then made casts of the shoe prints.

One of the techs mentioned to me that the tread looked like it belonged to an athletic shoe, cross-trainers or running shoes. There was a fairly good chance they could identify the brand.

With all that was happening at the house, I'd completely forgotten about my meeting with Chow and his lawyer until he rang me on my cell. I apologized and told him I would call him back later to reschedule. He also mentioned that Chow had made bail, but he assured me he wasn't a flight risk.

They all say that.

It was nearly three p.m. when the tech team began wrapping up. Lucy was due out of school. I told Po Po I would pick her up. After having Xiaolian snatched right out from under us, I had an overwhelming need to hug my daughter.

"Go on. I'll wait here until you get back," Kang said.

The walk wasn't far. Lucy was already waiting at our designated spot, and talking to one of her friends.

"Lucy," I called out.

She turned with a surprised look on her face. "What are you doing here?"

"I'm picking you up. Got a problem with that?" I leaned in and gave her a kiss on her head.

"No, it's okay. I thought Po Po was coming."

"Who's your friend?"

"This is Sasha."

"Hello," she said with a quick glance my way.

"I'll see you tomorrow," Lucy told her before walking with

me. "Don't you have to work today?" she asked as she aligned her steps so they matched mine.

"I do. I am. There's something I have to tell you. Xiaolian went missing today."

"She left?"

"That's what we're trying to find out. Someone who knows her might have taken her."

"Oh, I hope she's okay."

"Me too."

We walked hand in hand quietly for a bit. I guessed Lucy was thinking about Xiaolian. I knew I was.

"Mommy?"

"Yes."

"I have something I need to discuss with you."

"It sounds important."

"It is. As you know, my birthday is coming up."

Birthday? That's right. Jeez, how could that have slipped my mind? "I know that."

"I know you know. But listen to me. I've been thinking a lot about what gift you can give me."

"You have?" I asked, barely containing a chuckle.

"Yes. It's an important day in my life."

"And what has all of this serious thinking resulted in?"

"I want to get my ears pierced. Stop! Before you answer, I want you to take a deep breath and let it out slowly. I don't want your answer now. I want you to sleep on it. I want you to really think hard. Do you understand me?"

I could see she was dead serious, even though she stared at the ground as we walked. I dared not laugh and did my best to filter the words that next came out of my mouth.

"I understand. I'll give it my fairest consideration."

"Thank you, Mommy."

"So what brought this on?"

"It's something me and my friends have agreed to do. Everyone is supposed to go home and ask. Since my birthday is coming, I think it would make the most perfect of all gifts ever."

The remainder of the walk home, we let the subject of ear-piercing lay where we left it and talked about her day in school. She never brought up Xiaolian, and I had to wonder if it was because I was the only person who seemed to be obsessed with her or if it was because Lucy wasn't concerned. I leaned toward the former.

Xiaolian wasn't family. She was a part of an investigation I had invited into our home. Sure, she was nice and just a little girl. Her situation wasn't ideal. I'd like to think most people would have felt badly for her and taken her in for a few days.

But that wasn't the only reason I'd taken her in.

There were other reasons, arguably selfish in a way. I had wanted help with my investigation. I could benefit from Xiaolian staying with me. Now granted, I'd come across children who had been abandoned, beaten, and sexually abused by someone in the past. This wasn't my first rodeo. And sure, I felt bad. Who wouldn't? But I'd never felt a strong desire to take them into my home, even if I thought it could help with an investigation. I would just visit them at the shelter or wherever they were being housed if I needed to question them.

So why Xiaolian? What made her so special? Was the answer as simple as she looked like me? Perhaps. Or was it something bigger? Could it be that the whole suitcase situation had never felt right to me? Why stuff a girl into a piece of luggage and deliver her straight to the offices of the FBI if not to have her found and investigated?

I was deep in thought when Lucy tugged on my arm, directing me into our driveway.

"We're home," she sang.

Hearing Lucy say those two words, I wondered if Xiaolian had finally found her way home.

CHAPTER THIRTY-NINE

The forensics unit had already packed up and left before Lucy and I arrived. Po Po was sweeping the kitchen floor; she had prepared bite-sized sandwiches for Lucy's afterschool snack.

"Where's Kyle?" I asked her

"He working in the backyard."

I assumed what Po Po really meant to say was that he was relaxing on the back porch, but I was wrong. He was actually watering the hedges that surrounded my property.

"Are you my new grounds crew?" I called out from the porch.

Kang smiled at me and continued watering.

I walked over to him. "I didn't think my yard lacked in care, but I'm liking this side of you. When will you be back to mow?"

He smiled. "It seemed a little dry." He switched off the hose. "Nothing more to report aside from the shoe print. They recovered a few prints from the door. They also printed Po Po to rule her out."

"You know what Xiaolian's disappearance means?"

"That it could be a kidnapping, which will merit an investigation."

"Yup, the only problem is it doesn't look like she was taken by force."

"You don't know that," he said. "She was outside. She could have easily been overpowered, maybe even knocked out and quickly put into a vehicle out front."

"I realize that. It's just... how did this person know she was here with me? Only my team, the director at the shelter, and CPS were aware. That's not a lot of people." I shrugged. "Smells funny."

"Especially if she went willingly. Let's knock on doors and see where that leads us."

Of course, talking to the neighbors led us nowhere. No one had seen Xiaolian or noticed a strange car or person snooping around. There were not many people who were home at the time—most were working.

On the way back to my house, I put a call in to Reilly and gave him an update.

"A shoe print? Not much to go on, but you got your wish, Abby. Keep me posted on your findings."

We stopped on the sidewalk in front of my house.

"You think the same person who had dropped her off might have had a change of heart and came back for her?" Kang asked.

"Maybe, but according to Xiaolian, she remembers seeing Chow's tattoo right before she got into the suitcase." I crossed my arms over my chest.

"Maybe she's mistaken. Chow could very well have passed her off to another person."

I nodded. "You know what really bothers me? Is that they

knew she was here. Makes me think someone might have been watching Xiaolian the entire time."

Kang rested his hands on his hips. "You mean from the moment she arrived at your home?" He looked up and down the street. "If that's true, they could have been casing your place and waiting for the right moment."

A shiver ran throughout my body. This wasn't the first time some psycho had been watching my home. There was even a break-in once. But in all those instances, I knew I was chasing a dangerous person and that there was a chance they might come after my family or me. But Xiaolian never put me in that mindset. I never once thought her staying with us would pose a threat. Maybe I had grossly miscalculated.

"But why? Why drop her off and then take her back?" I asked.

"Maybe she contacted someone," Kang said. "It would explain how someone found her and why there was no break-in or struggle."

"Well, seeing that she was smuggled into the country, she either contacted one of our four Stanford geniuses, or she contacted the person who dropped her off at our offices, if such a person exists. Let's pay a visit to Chow. He needs to start talking."

CHAPTER FORTY

I WAS GLAD I DROVE. I felt the need to let out some aggression, and getting behind the wheel of my Charger did just that. I punched the gas pedal. The rear wheels chirped, and the force pushed me back into my seat. I loved that feeling.

"Easy, slick," Kang said.

"Sorry, do I need to find a bathroom so you can clean your shorts?"

"You're funny... funny looking." Kang slapped his thigh repeatedly. "I got you on that one."

"If you say so."

"But seriously," he said, still smiling, "what makes you think Chow will talk to us without his lawyer?"

"I don't. But if he refuses, I'll make him call his lawyer over to his place while we wait."

Fifteen minutes later, we were standing outside Chow's apartment, knocking on the door.

"Darren Chow. This is Agent Kane with the FBI. We'd like to ask you a few questions."

No response. I knocked again and repeated my request but still nothing.

"Maybe he's not home," Kang said.

I turned the doorknob just to see if the door was locked. It wasn't. I looked up at Kang. "Should we? He might be in trouble. Perhaps a quick peek just to be sure he's okay?"

Kang nodded. "Good idea."

We entered the apartment.

"Darren Chow. This is the FBI. Are you home? We found your front door unlocked."

The living room was empty and looked exactly as it had at our last visit.

"Did he even come back here?" I asked.

"The bedroom door is closed. He might be sleeping."

I started to head that way, but Kang stopped me and motioned to let him enter first. I rolled my eyes. "Seriously?"

"What? I'm eager. I want to go in first. That's all."

"Whatever." I stepped to the side, and he entered the room first.

Inside, there was nothing to be afraid of. No threats to be had.

"I didn't see that coming," Kang said.

"Me either." I moved in for a closer look. Chow lay on his back with his eyes closed and a gunshot hole in the middle of his forehead.

"Looks like he was shot at close range," I said. "Whoever did this probably snuck in while he was sleeping."

"I didn't notice any signs of forced entry at his front door," Kang said.

"No deadbolt. They could have easily picked the lock."

Kang leaned in for a closer look as well. "Doesn't look like he's been dead that long. Blood hasn't coagulated."

"They weren't interested in taking anything either. He's wearing a nice watch. This has all the signs of a professional hit."

"They came in, did the job, and left."

"Dammit," I said, resting my hands on my hips. "Chow was our connection to the person responsible for Xiaolian."

"That could be the reason. Maybe whoever took Xiaolian from the house is responsible; they felt the need to eliminate ties."

I called Agents Hansen and Pratt and told them to check on the other three. If a connection did exist between the person who'd killed Chow and taken Xiaolian, then the other three members of his crew might be in danger as well. Kang alerted SFPD.

While we waited for the forensics team to arrive, we looked around the apartment. We saw no signs of another person being there, or of a struggle. A shoulder bag lay flat on the floor near the couch. I peeked inside and spotted a tablet.

"We might be able to pull something off of this," I said, pointing to the tablet. "Maybe he emailed his customer. I don't see a phone lying around, do you?"

"Let me check the bedroom."

Kang returned. "There's a burner cell phone in his front pocket. I'll have it added to our evidence list."

Once forensics arrived, Kang and I questioned the neighbors on Chow's floor. Most of them weren't home, and the few who were hadn't heard anything suspicious. One even mentioned that he knew what a gunshot sounded like and would have definitely recognized that sound if he'd heard it.

Nothing was going our way. And it was about to get worse. Hansen called to let us know that he had tracked down Sticks.

"Does he know anything about Chow?" I asked.

"Sticks is dead, Abby."

Ten minutes later, Pratt called. "I'm at Lim and Dickson's place. They're both dead. Gunshot to the head."

Not only was Xiaolian missing, the four responsible for smuggling her into the country had all been executed in the span of a couple hours.

"Everyone connected has been wiped out," Kang said.

"And it might not be over." I pulled out my phone and dialed Rosales. "It's Agent Kane. Where are those girls from the shipping container being held?"

CHAPTER FORTY-ONE

Alonzo told Walter to make a right at the next intersection. He continued to stare at the map on his phone, watching the blue dot move closer and closer to the pin he had dropped.

"Here," he said as he pointed at a building with colorful murals painted on it.

Walter parked the Monte Carlo outside the building. Alonzo reloaded a magazine and snapped it back into his handgun. They looked at each other, nodded, and then exited the vehicle.

Alonzo went into the building first. There was a young woman sitting at the reception desk and two other women sitting on a nearby couch, looking over paperwork. Walter kept an eye on the last two. Alonzo removed his cell phone and produced pictures of the girls from the container.

"Where are they?" he asked the receptionist, shoving his cell phone into her face.

"Can I ask who you are?" she said with a smile. She still hadn't noticed the gun in his other hand.

"Where are they?" he asked once more.

"I have to log you in first. It's required of all visitors."

Alonzo looked back at Walter, and he nodded.

Alonzo raised his gun and pulled the trigger. Her head snapped back before her body slumped in the chair.

The sound of the gunshot jerked the women sitting on the couch to attention. One lady opened her mouth, preparing to sound a screaming alarm. Walter shot her before she finished drawing her breath.

Blood splatter covered the lady sitting next to her. Her eyes locked on the bleeding mess. She struggled to breath, choking with each gasp.

Walter walked up to her, raised his gun so the barrel was inches from her temple. The woman still hadn't been able to tear her gaze away from the dead woman. He pulled the trigger and walked away.

The brothers entered a short hallway where there were three rooms. The two on the left had the doors shut. Walter peeled off toward them. Alonzo checked the room with the door open. It was an office.

Inside he found a woman talking quietly on the phone. The last word he heard her say before shooting her was, "Hurry."

Alonzo heard his brother fire his weapon. He walked back into the hall just as Walter exited a bedroom.

"Done," he said as he showed Alonzo the picture of the girl he'd found.

They both eyed the stairwell leading up to a second floor.

Forensics had yet to show up to Chow's apartment, but a couple of officers with SFPD had. They secured the crime scene, and we headed over to women's shelter.

On the way over, I called the shelter. "No one's answering," I said.

"You really think the girls are in danger?" Kang asked.

"I'm not sure, but just to be safe, we should have them moved to a safer environment until we can figure out what the hell is going on here."

The shelter was about a ten-minute drive from our location, so we arrived fairly quickly. I parked behind a gold Monte Carlo. That was when we heard a scream from inside.

Walter and Alonzo stood at the top of the stairs, staring down a long hall with multiple rooms on each side. Some doors were closed; others were open.

Alonzo stepped into the first room on the right. There were two bunk beds and four girls. He looked at each one carefully, even double-checking the photos on his phone. He then shot the girl on the top right bunk. Dead. One of the girls in the room screamed.

As he headed into the next room on the right, he heard Walter fire multiple times.

Alonzo found five girls in the next room. Again he carefully studied their faces and compared them to the photos on his phone. Two of the girls didn't match. Two of them did—he shot them right away. He had trouble IDing the fifth girl. He wasn't positive if she was a match with one of the girls in the photo. She sort of looked like one of them.

He moved in closer.

The girl held her hands up in front of her defensively. Tears trailed the sides of her cheeks.

Alonzo sat on the bed next to her.

The girl shivered as if she were standing naked in the middle of a winter storm. He still wasn't sure. Another shot rang out in the background. The girl let out a scream and cried harder. She begged him not to hurt her. Alonzo continued to compare her to a photo. He even held his phone up next to her face.

He raised his gun.

His eyes shifted back and forth between her and the photo.

He breathed in and breathed out slowly.

He pursed his lips as he mulled.

Slowly his finger edged back on the trigger.

Walter entered the room. "How many?"

Alonzo answered, "I took care of four."

Walter then said, "We're done. She's not one of them."

Alonzo peered harder into the girl's eyes. He still hadn't lowered his gun, the barrel inches from her face. "Are you sure?"

"I took care of seven. It's over."

Alonzo lowered his gun. "Sorry," he told the girl.

Before heading inside, we called in the shooting and requested backup, but we couldn't just sit back and wait it out. We had to move in. We heard more screaming. And gunshots.

The first thing we saw after entering the building was the young receptionist. She was slumped over her desk, a pool of blood spread outward from her head.

"Psst," Kang said, gesturing toward the two motionless women on the couch. He hurried over to them and checked for pulses. He shook his head.

I found Massey, the director of the shelter, in her office. She was missing the top of her forehead. I drew a deep breath and gripped the handle on my weapon more tightly.

Kang appeared at the entrance to Massey's office with two young girls by his side, each hanging on to him as if their lives depended on it. Which was entirely possible. "There's another girl in the room next door. She's down."

"The shooter might still be here," I whispered as I pointed upward.

Slowly we walked back out to the hallway. I took point. Kang was right behind me with the two little ones, who surprisingly were maintaining their composure. The stairs were the only way up to the second floor. I stopped at the corner and peeked around. Empty.

"It's clear," I said softly.

Kang pointed to the front door that was still wide open and told the girls to run outside

I moved to the foot of the stairs, gun out in front. Step by step, I climbed as I peered upward. I crouched lower when I reached the landing, listening. I could hear crying. And then a loud shriek that sent a chill racing throughout my body.

As I neared the top of the stairs, I could see down the hall. I still heard crying. Kang moved up next to me. He motioned for me to cover the rooms on the right; he would take the ones on the left.

Cautiously we moved ahead.

My heart thumped loudly. It had been a while since I had been in a position like this. Images of Lucy, Ryan, and Po Po popped into my head. I had a family. They counted on me being alive. *Don't get shot, Abby.*

With my back against the wall, I moved forward. Across the hall, Kang did the same. I could see inside the rooms on Kang's side before he could, and vice versa, which allowed us to provide an extra layer of protection before just bolting into a room. This was our dance, and we performed it flawlessly.

I peered inside the room Kang was approaching and saw a girl lying face down on the floor, motionless. I nodded for him to enter the room, and he gave me the okay to enter the room on my side.

I found two bunk beds. Two girls were dead. Two were alive.

I hurried the girls out of the room, telling them to run downstairs and get out of the building. Kang entered the hallway with one girl and sent her on her way.

We continued on to the next two rooms. In my heart, I hoped I wouldn't find any more victims. That hope faded quickly as I spotted another motionless girl in the room Kang was nearing. There were more to be found in the room on my side of the hall.

With each room we cleared, the tally of deaths grew. It was clear that some girls were spared, even Asian ones, and some weren't. My guess was that the girls who'd been shot were part of the group smuggled into the US on that container; at least age-wise they were in line with what Hansen had told me. I wasn't that familiar with their faces.

The girls who survived were in a state of shock, crying and unable to move or speak on their own.

There was only one way out, and no one had snuck past us. *Where are you?*

Kang and I stood in the hall. Two rooms left to clear. The one on my side had its door closed. The one on Kang's side didn't. We dealt with his room first. Two dead.

We then faced the closed door of the last room. The shooter had to be inside. I leaned in and listened. I heard nothing. Kang wanted to wait for backup. The sound of sirens grew louder. The smart thing to do would have been to let a tactical team take down the room.

But that's not how I roll.

I adjusted my ballistics vest and motioned for Kang to ready himself. I soft-checked the doorknob. It was unlocked. He leaned up against the wall next to the door. I stood on the opposite side of the door. With the door sandwiched between us, I reached for the knob once more.

One.

I raised my weapon.

Two.

I braced myself.

Three.

CHAPTER FORTY-TWO

INSIDE WE FOUND A SINGLE GIRL. She sat on the floor in the corner of the room with her knees pulled up against her chest and her arms wrapped around them. I checked on her while Kang inspected an open window. He peered outside.

"I don't see anyone," he said. "If he did exit from here, he probably climbed down. It's doable."

He brought his head back inside.

"Are you okay, sweetie?" I asked the frightened girl.

She didn't respond, just rocked back and forth.

"Listen, you're safe now. No one will hurt you."

"I'm heading back downstairs to meet with the tact team."

I nodded and then helped the girl to her feet. "Are you okay?"

Finally, she spoke: "I think so."

I looked her over and didn't see any visible injuries. Right away I knew she wasn't with the group of girls from the container—she was Latino, probably no older than ten.

I pointed at the window. "Did you see someone climb out?"

She nodded. "A bad man. He was very scary."

"I know, but I'll tell you something. I won't stop chasing after him until I catch him and lock him up in jail. Can you tell me what he looked like?"

"He looked Japanese."

"Hmm, do you think he might have been Chinese?" I figured she probably couldn't tell the difference, but being that the girls were from China, I had to assume the person who came after them might be Chinese as well. Of course, I could just as easily have been wrong.

"Maybe, I'm not sure."

"Okay, that's very good information. Can you tell me what kind of clothes he wore?"

"He had black jeans and a long-sleeve shirt—a nice one that you can wear to a party. It was black with swirly red lines."

"Did he have a beard or a mustache?" I rubbed my chin.

"No."

"What about tattoos?"

"I was too scared to look at him. I'm sorry."

"It's okay, sweetie. You're doing fine."

I helped her to her feet.

"Where are we going?"

"Outside. I want a doctor to look at you and make sure you're not hurt. Can you do something for me?"

She nodded.

"When we leave the room, it's very important that you look straight ahead. I want you to focus on the stairs; don't look in the rooms. Can you do that?"

"Yes."

"Good. We'll both do it together."

We exited the room, and I hurried her down the hall.

"Look at the stairs, sweetie. Keep looking straight ahead. You can do it."

I glanced off to the side and saw a body. My heart ached for these girls. Down the stairs we went.

"Keep looking straight ahead," I repeated. I used my body to block her view of the two dead women on the couch.

As we exited the building, we bumped into the tactical unit. "Anybody else inside?" the commander asked.

"I don't know. I can't be sure we covered every room."

"We'll do a full sweep."

SFPD had arrived on the scene and began securing the perimeter. There were two ambulances, and the paramedics were attending to the girls we'd told to leave the building. I walked the last girl over to the paramedics before I found Kang.

"Do you know if we have all the girls accounted for?" I asked.

"I think so," he said. "I can't be sure. When I got outside, a few were standing by that tree over there. I haven't questioned them yet." He rested his hands on his waist. "We got fifteen bodies here plus Chow and his crew. A bloody massacre."

"And according to the girl I brought out, one person is behind it, or at least what happened here. She saw a man climb out the window."

"Just one guy?"

"That's what she says. She also said he looked Japanese and was dressed nicely."

We walked around the side of the building, careful to keep an eye out for shoe prints or anything that could ID our shooter. Behind the building, we located the window that belonged to the last room we were in. It wasn't very high up, maybe twenty feet. A person could easily have climbed or dropped down.

Kang peered at the grass below the window. "I don't see any impressions."

"Maybe he climbed down," I said. "There." I pointed.

The paint on the building had seen a lot of years, as it was cracked in many places, but there was an area where a bunch of it had flaked off. We examined the ground below the window more closely and saw the paint flakes.

"He definitely climbed down," Kang said.

"So we have a hit placed on everyone associated with the smuggling of the girls, including the girls who were smuggled," I said.

"Don't forget the workers at the shelter," Kang said.

"Collateral damage. The shooter could have shot all of the girls who were here, but he only shot the ones from that container."

"He had a list and did his best to stick to it."

"I think so. Whoever is responsible found out Chow and his crew got pinched. They didn't want them talking."

"About what? I didn't think we learned much of anything from them outside of their operations," Kang said.

"Obviously there's something they know that wasn't revealed to us. Chow kept his mouth shut; he might have held information the others weren't aware of. He was also the only one who'd been in contact with the person who hired them to transport Xiaolian. That's got to be the connection."

"So this person figured the only way to stop the flow of information is to eliminate everyone involved."

"Better late than never," I said as I shifted my weight from one foot to another.

"The only other two people associated with the smuggling ring are Medina and Watts and they're currently in custody. So are the two men who resupplied the ship in Honolulu. Lucky for them, or they would most likely be dead."

"Still, the pieces don't add up." I folded my arms across my chest. "If we think the person responsible for hiring Chow to transport Xiaolian is the one who ordered the hit on all of these people, are they also responsible for Xiaolian's disappearance?"

"You think she's dead?" Kang asked.

"It's a strong possibility, but if she was part of the hit, it doesn't follow the MO. All of the others were shot dead where they stood. She wasn't."

"Well, considering we think she wasn't taken from your house by force, this tells me she either knew the person or didn't feel threatened."

"So did the person who ordered her transported in the first place come back for her?"

"Maybe." Kang scratched the back of his head. "Seems like whenever we think we have this figured out, we don't."

"Well, if there's one thing we know, whoever hired Chow holds the answer to a lot of what's happened here."

By the time we made our way back to the front of the building, the first of the media vans had shown up. There would be no way to contain this—multiple homicides across the city, and involving children. The story screamed up-to-the-minute coverage.

CHAPTER FORTY-THREE

XIAOLIAN WINCED AS SHE SLEPT. The familiar scenes from her past dreams had returned.

She's walking down the hallway, alone at first, until a man in a white jacket overtakes her. He grabs hold of her hand and leads her forward.

"Hurry, we're late," he says.

She still can't see his face, but she follows. Two men wearing similar jackets walk toward them. They're looking at a file as they discuss something.

The man stops in front of a door. This time she looks up at him and is able to stare directly into his eyes.

"Are you ready?" he asks.

Xiaolian woke with a gasp and short breaths quickly followed. *Where am I?* It took a moment or so for her to remember, but once she did, she began to calm. She blinked repeatedly and then yawned. The curtains were drawn across the window, but bits of sunlight snuck in near the bottom of the drapes. Still, the room was fairly dark.

She reached out for a nearby lamp on the bedside table, only to realize a plastic strap had secured her wrist to the bed. Her other hand was free so she rolled over to her side and used it to switch on the lamp.

The small lamp cast a warm glow across the room, illuminating two twin beds, a dresser with a TV on top of it, and a small, round table with two chairs. There was a door leading to a small bathroom and another that led out of the room.

Her tongue stuck to her mouth, causing her to crave something cool to drink. She drew a deep breath and stretched her legs. She looked over at the clock; she had been asleep for a few hours, but it felt longer.

A few moments later, the sound of a key being inserted into a lock grabbed her attention. The door swung inward, and the outline of a man stood in the doorway. He quickly shut the door behind him and turned the deadbolt to the locked position.

"You're up," he said in Chinese. "Are you hungry? Of course you are."

He set two white paper bags down on the table and then dug into the front pocket of his pants and removed something.

"I'm sorry about your wrist. I hope you understand."

He sat on the edge of the bed next to her. Even though she had awoken alone in a strange room and was tied to a bed, she didn't feel the least bit threatened by him, not even when he produced a pocketknife from his pocket.

While he used it to cut her wrist free, her eyes traced his features: brown eyes, short salt-and-pepper hair, bushy eyebrows, a brown mole below the left corner of his bottom lip, sunspots on the top of his hands. These were familiar characteristics. The only thing missing was a long, white jacket. There was no mistake in her mind. The man from her dreams had found her.

CHAPTER FORTY-FOUR

KANG and I were still at the women's shelter when Sokolov and Bennie arrived. "Tell me you guys didn't catch the collar for this one," he said.

"It's the captain's gift to us," Sokolov responded. "Abby, you weren't kidding when you said you would find a way to involve us."

"Sorry I kept my word. Are you guys handling all of the bodies?"

He shook his head. "Just the fifteen here," he said with a sarcastic bent.

I looked at Bennie. "Welcome to San Francisco. Come on. We'll walk you through the crime scene."

We filled them in on what had transpired from the moment we arrived, to entering the building, to clearing the rooms.

"This is the window where our shooter escaped?" Sokolov asked, sticking his head out, careful not to touch anything as CSI had yet to process the room.

"I found one of the survivors, a Latino girl, in this room. She saw an Asian male who was 'dressed for a party'—her words—

climb out that window. She might be able to recall more details given some time."

"We heard shots just as we arrived," Kang added. "The shooter was definitely on the premises at that time."

We walked them outside and around to the back of the building where I pointed out the chipped paint. "Looks fresh and in line with someone climbing down the side of the building," I said.

As we walked back around to the front of the building, Sokolov said, "Not much to go on."

I agreed with him. Kang and I were just as deep in this mess as he and Bennie were.

Sokolov looked at the various first-responder vehicles parked on the street. "Is that your vehicle there?"

"Yes."

"Do you remember if there was another vehicle out front when you arrived?"

"Now that you mention it, we did park behind another car. It was gold in color, faded though."

Kang started nodding. "You're right. An older make..." He snapped his finger. "It was a Monte Carlo."

"Gold Monte Carlo. You positive?" Sokolov asked.

We both nodded. "Definitely an older model; the one with the long hood," I said.

"I'm guessing it wasn't here when you guys came back out," Bennie said.

"Kang, you got out here first," I said as I turned to him.

He crinkled his brow and thought for a second or two. "No, it was gone. We were inside maybe ten, fifteen minutes at the most before I came back outside."

"Our shooter uses the window to escape while you two are

busy clearing rooms. He comes around front, gets back into his vehicle, and drives off. Bold son of bitch," Bennie said.

"Okay, we're looking for a gold Monte Carlo," Sokolov said.

"My cousin restored a car like this. It has a hood that sticks out for miles with a short behind. The make you guys are talking about came out in '75, '76, and '77. They don't blend easily, especially with a gold paint job and an Asian driver. No offense," Bennie said, looking at Kang. "Usually people of my skin color, brown pride, are sitting behind the wheel."

"It's too bad video cameras aren't standard issue on your vehicles," Sokolov noted.

I had to agree with Sokolov. Having that footage would have revealed the make, model, license plate, and most importantly, our shooter. Instead, we would have to go about this the old-fashioned way, piecing together bits and pieces until we had the full picture.

"Is there anybody else you guys can think of who could potentially be on this hit list?" Bennie asked.

It dawned on me then that Sokolov and Bennie wouldn't have known about Xiaolian being missing. "Someone grabbed Xiaolian from my house earlier today."

"You're kidding, right?" Bennie asked.

I told them what we knew. It wasn't until I found myself repeating the details that I began to realize she might very well be dead.

"She could be dead, but why not just do her right there?" Sokolov asked.

"That's the dilemma we were wrestling with earlier, before you got here," I said.

"There could be two people working together," Bennie said.

"One person is dispatched to grab Xiaolian. The other person is sent to eliminate everyone involved."

I bit down on my bottom lip. There was something about Bennie's words that had me thinking in a different direction. "You know, we're all assuming these people were killed because of their involvement with the smuggling deal."

"Well, yeah, they were," Kang said.

"I agree but hear me out. Forget about involvement. Xiaolian has always been the odd person throughout this investigation. I'm thinking maybe these people weren't killed for their involvement but rather that they're all witnesses to Xiaolian."

"So whoever orchestrated the hits wants to keep her a secret?" Kang asked.

"That's an interesting thought," Sokolov said.

I clucked my tongue as I considered the possibilities. "There's one last person connected that we haven't spoken to."

"Who's that?" Kang asked.

"The lawyer."

CHAPTER FORTY-FIVE

XIAOLIAN and the man sat at the table. A hanging lamp lit the area. Their dinner consisted of hamburgers, chili-cheese fries, and colas. They ate mostly in silence.

The fast-food joint he'd visited earlier had a television in the dining area, and he saw the media coverage of the shooting spree. The mayor of San Francisco stood on the steps of City Hall and gave a statement condemning the massacre. He assured the citizens of the city that SFPD, the sheriff's department, and the FBI were all working together to find the person responsible. A graphic along the bottom of screen had put the tally so far at nineteen people shot dead. In order to lessen Xiaolian's exposure to what had taken place, he kept the television in the room turned off.

"How do you feel?" he asked.

"I'm okay," she answered. "At first I couldn't remember anything, but now it's much better."

He finished the last bite of his burger and wiped his mouth. From a suitcase in the corner he removed a small, black bag.

"Come over to the bed," he said.

She slid off the chair and took a seat at the edge of the mattress. He removed a blood-pressure kit from the bag and monitored her pressure. He checked her temperature, and her glands for swelling. He used a stethoscope to listen to her heart and her breathing. He refrained from saying anything while he examined her.

"Am I okay?" she asked after he removed the stethoscope from his ears.

"Yes, you're fine. Eventually all of your memory will come back. It's temporary." He returned the medical equipment to the black bag. "Did you enjoy staying with the lady and her family?"

She nodded. "They were nice. Her name is Abby, and she works for the police. She has a son and his name is Ryan. Her daughter's name is Lucy. They were all very nice to me, especially Po Po. I think she's Abby's mom."

"She's her mother-in-law."

"How do you know?"

"I've known about Abby for a very long time."

Her eyes widened. "Really? Why do you know her? Is she from the same place as us?"

"No, she isn't."

"Why do you know her then? Are you friends?"

He opened his mouth but stopped short of answering. He took a moment to think and then said, "Everyone back home misses you."

"I miss them too."

"Do you remember leaving?"

Her gaze fell to the carpet. "Bits and pieces."

"Do you remember anything about our home?"

"I remember you. I remember some of my friends and our classes, but that's it. I'm worried I won't ever remember."

"Don't. I assure you that your memory loss is only temporary."

"I hope so. I really want to remember. It's frustrating not knowing the answer when someone asks a question."

"I know."

"Are you here to take me back?"

"Do you want to go back?"

She thought about his question before answering with a shrug. "Maybe. Am I in trouble?"

"Does it matter to you?"

"I don't want anyone to be mad at me."

He rubbed his chin as he considered his next words. "I'm not here to take you back."

"Why did you come here?"

"I needed to make sure you were safe and all right."

"I'm okay. Will I live with Abby now?"

"I don't know."

"Does she not like me anymore? Is that why you've come?"

"No, it's not that. I'm here because I wanted to make sure you were okay. That's all."

"Will you leave me soon?"

"Not just yet. It's not safe for you right now."

She drew a sharp breath. "I knew it. It's the chief. He's angry with me, isn't he?"

The man didn't answer her, and not because he was at a loss for words. In fact, he had much to tell her, but the timing wasn't right. What he had to say would only confuse her. He felt she needed to regain all of her memory in order for her to understand what was happening.

For the time being, his priority was keeping her out of sight. It was the only way to guarantee her safety. Until then, the motel they were hiding in would be their home.

"How long will you stay with me?" she asked.

"I'm not sure. Do you want me to stay?"

"Yes. It's nice knowing someone. Maybe we can live together."

"Maybe."

He watched her chew on her lower lip. He sensed what was coming next.

"Can I ask you something?" Her voice was meek, a sign of uncertainty with him.

Of course he knew what she was about to ask. It was inevitable. His only surprise was that she hadn't asked the question sooner.

"Why do I look like Abby?"

CHAPTER FORTY-SIX

"Man, I feel bad for Sokolov and Bennie," Kang said as he stared out his window at the passing scenery. "That's a lot of bodies they need to clear."

"It is, but at least they're all connected," I said as I shifted gears. "It would be a tougher one if they were unrelated homicides."

"Still..."

"I hear you."

Kang flicked his thumb across the screen of his cell phone. "I'm looking at the lawyer's address on a map. It seems he works out of his house."

"Really?"

"The building for the address we have looks residential."

"I'm guessing he also has one client—Chow. What's the lawyer's name again?" I asked.

"Wen Yu."

"That's right."

"Name like that isn't that common here. Most likely the guy was born in China and immigrated later."

"Is he in the Inner Richmond area?"

"You would think, but he's in fog land—Outer Sunset area."

I looked over at Kang. "Are you serious?"

"This is the address Hansen texted me."

A lot of middle- and upper-class Chinese families lived in areas known as the Inner and Outer Richmond area. I had just assumed if his office wasn't in Chinatown proper or the Financial District, it was in the Richmond areas.

I drove west on Geary Boulevard until it ended at Ocean Beach and then headed south along the coast and into the Sunset neighborhood. No sooner had we passed by the western edge of the Golden Gate Park, visibility began to drop dramatically. I downshifted and switched my fog lights on.

The Sunset neighborhood received the least amount of sun in San Francisco, but it was relatively safe and affordable. A lot of families chose to live there despite the foggy conditions year round. I couldn't do it. Too dreary for my taste; though perfect for that vampire family from the Twilight series if they ever wanted to relocate.

"Make a left on Sloat," Kang said. "He's on Crestlake Drive, near Stern Grove."

Stern Grove was a fairly large recreational park—lots of trees and trails. Its claim to fame was a large amphitheater, complete with stone-wall terraces for seating. It had been hosting shows for decades.

The southwest area of the park butted right up against Yu's property, a single-family ranch home. Even with the thick fog, I could make out the outline of the tall eucalyptus trees that dominated the flora of the park behind his house.

I parked along the curb in front of the house. An older

model Mercedes sedan was parked in the driveway. Its black paint job had long lost its sheen.

"I hope that car is a signal that he's home," Kang said.

The area was unusually quiet for the time of the day—dusk. "I don't know how people can live out here," I said as I exited the vehicle. "It's totally zombie-apocalypse-like."

"Two words," Kang said. "Affordable housing."

We made the walk up the paved driveway, the click-clacking of our shoes the only audible sound outside of the change jingling in Kang's pants.

He rang the doorbell. We waited. He rang it once more. At that point I began looking through the windows.

"See anything?" he asked.

"It's dark inside. I don't see any lights on. Maybe he isn't home. Try ringing him."

Kang dialed Yu's number on his phone, but nobody picked up.

"Keep trying," I said. I walked to the side of the house. A tall, wooden fence separated his property from the house next door, but there was no gate stopping someone from following the fence to his backyard.

"Maybe he's out back and can't hear our knocking."

Kang followed me. He still had his cell phone pressed up against his ear when we passed a window and heard the ringing of a cell phone.

"It's like stereo," Kang said, lowering his phone. "That's his phone ringing."

Even though the curtain was drawn on the window, we could definitely hear the phone. I rapped my knuckles on the windowpane. "Mr. Yu. It's the FBI. We need to ask you a few questions."

No one responded, and the phone inside continued to ring.

We moved around to the rear of the house. There was a covered patio and a small patch of grass, which led to a wooden fence separating the property from the park.

"Look," Kang said, pointing at the sliding glass door. It was cracked open a few inches.

"He's not responding to our questions. We have reasonable cause to think he might be in danger," I said.

I drew my weapon and entered the home with Kang right behind me. Just inside was an open kitchen and small dining table. The décor looked as if it hadn't changed since the house was built: wood-stained cabinets in the kitchen with yellow linoleum flooring and pea-green shag carpeting in the living room.

Kang motioned to me that he was going to clear the bedrooms and then headed toward a darkened hall. I nodded and headed toward the room where the phone had been ringing. The door was closed, so I soft-checked the knob. It wasn't locked. I pushed the door open while at the same time stepping back behind the cover of the wall.

Silence.

I peeked around the corner and saw Mr. Yu sitting in a leather executive chair behind a large desk. His eyes were closed and his forearms were resting on the desktop with his hands clasped together.

Maybe he's a heavy sleeper.

"Mr. Yu," I said as I carefully approached him.

He looked peaceful as opposed to large-hole-in-the-middle-of-his-forehead dead.

If he were dead, the MO didn't fit.

"Mr. Yu," I said once more as I walked around the desk.

I reached out with the barrel of my handgun and nudged him in the shoulder. His body fell forward, hitting the desktop with a soft thud.

"Is he dead?" Kang stood in the doorway. "The rest of the house is empty."

"He's not breathing." I checked for a pulse and found none.

"Doesn't look like he was shot." Kang walked around the desk for a closer look at the body.

"Yeah, strange. Maybe he died of natural causes. A heart attack or something along those lines, and this is just a coincidence."

"That would be strange if it were."

I scanned the desktop for a note or anything that might reveal what he'd been working on in his office. There was nothing aside from the corner of a yellow legal pad sticking out from under his body. I lifted him up just enough to see that there was no writing on the pad.

"You know, I find it weird that there's nothing in his home office that conveys that he actually works here. It's more like a den where he might sit to open his daily mail."

"I thought the same thing. No filing cabinets. No paperwork. No landline."

Kang called Yu's phone again. The ringing came from the man's pants pocket.

"Maybe forensics will be able to tell us more."

"I'll call it in," Kang said.

With the exception of all of the doors and windows, only the sliding door was unlocked; and Yu certainly hadn't died in the same way Chow and the others had. Our minds were boggled, to say the least.

While we waited for CSI to arrive, Kang mentioned something that I should have considered long ago. If our thinking was that everyone who had contact with Xiaolian was potentially on the hit list, then my family should be on that list as well.

CHAPTER FORTY-SEVEN

As we raced across town, Kang called for SFPD to send a unit over to my address. This was the second time Kang had to make that call in the course of a day.

"I can't frickin believe I didn't consider this. Just when I thought I had this mom crap down, I blow it in a major way."

Ever since my husband was murdered and I inherited sole responsibility for two young children and an elderly mother-in-law, I'd been learning how to parent on the fly. And I wasn't always successful, especially with my profession.

Part of the reason for moving the family from Hong Kong to the States was to leave that baggage behind and start with a clean slate. The new job with the FBI was supposed to place me on mostly white-collar crimes—financial. But there I was, back in the thick of investigating violent crimes and placing my family in danger as a result. Oh, it wasn't the first time. That would be too perfect. And my life was anything but.

"Hey, this isn't a reflection on your parenting skills. You're in the middle of a huge investigation. We've got nineteen dead bodies. A madman on the run. A million things are running through our heads."

"And yet you still thought of them before I did. Dammit!"

"We're a team, Abby. I can think of some stuff too, you know."

"I know, I know, it's just that... well, you know how much I struggle with juggling work and family."

"I get it. And I for one think you're doing a terrific job. You need to cut yourself some slack. And anyway, this is a precaution. I honestly think if this guy had the knowledge of where all these individuals were, he would have known Xiaolian was staying with you and hit your place first."

I wanted Kang to be right, but my gut told me the opposite. When we reached the house, a squad car was already parked in my driveway.

"Everything's fine. All three are accounted for," one of the officers said.

I breathed a sigh of relief and thanked them before heading inside.

"Mommy! You're home!" Lucy hopped off the couch and gave me a hug.

"Where's Po Po?"

"In the kitchen."

"And your brother?"

"Taking a shower. Why are the police here?"

"We're staying in a hotel tonight. I want you to go upstairs and pack your suitcase, the small one. While you're up there, tell your brother to do the same and then meet me back down here." I patted her butt, sending her off. "And don't dilly dally."

Kang entered the house. "Po Po's cooking," he said, sniffing the air.

"We'll have to pack up dinner to go. I've got the kids getting their things. I think it's best they stay in a hotel for a few days."

"I wonder if we should have a team watching your house, just in case our guy shows up," Kang said.

"You just said it was unlikely this guy knows about Xiaolian staying here. You trying to give me an ulcer or something?"

He shrugged. "I know, and it's probably nothing, but if we're clearing your house out, why not give the impression they're still here? Leave the lights on, the TV, and then have a team watch the place, just in case. It might be worth it for a couple of hours."

"What, like a squad car out front? That would just scare him off."

"Forget about SFPD. Hansen and Pratt can watch the place."

I thought about it for a second or two. "Do it."

Kang made the call while I went to break the news to Po Po. She didn't seem bothered. If she was, she hid it well.

"Let me pack up the food," I said.

"It's okay. I can do."

"No, let me do it. You go and pack some things."

A little later I checked the family into a suite at the Fairmont on California Street. Kang was on the phone with Reilly, briefing him about the lawyer, and said he'd wait in the lobby.

Once settled in the room, I helped Po Po unpack dinner. She had prepared beef and broccoli, shrimp lo mein, pork fried rice, and stir-fried veggies. Nothing too elaborate.

"Aren't you eating with us?" Lucy asked me.

"Maybe later. I need to take care of something first. It does smell good though."

"It's excellent," she said. "You really should eat what Po Po cooked while it's warm. Plus it's even better in a hotel." Lucy raised her fork triumphantly. "I like being on vacation."

"We're not on vacation," Ryan said. "We're in a safe house."

"Ryan!" I said quickly.

"What? It's true. You work for the FBI, and sometimes your work spills over and it affects us. I know what's happening. Xiaolian's missing and you think she's connected to the—"

"Enough!" I cocked an eyebrow. It was the only sign Ryan needed in order to understand that uttering another word in front of Lucy would not bode well for him. The potential danger to my family wasn't something I wanted to broadcast to Lucy in its raw format. It would only give her nightmares. I was the parent. He was the child. Therefore, I controlled the dialogue.

"What's happening?" Lucy asked. "I want to know. I'm older now. It's not fair Ryan gets to know and not me."

"No one is keeping anything from you, sweetie. We're staying here for a few days because there's a bad man in town who is hurting people. Everyone is staying indoors."

"Did he hurt Xiaolian?"

"We don't think so, but we're looking for her just in case."

"But where did she go?"

"We don't know."

I gave Ryan a comforting squeeze on his shoulder just to let him know I loved him. I didn't blame the kid for the words that came out of his mouth. He was old enough to understand the nature of my job. Everything he said was true, but he had no filter. For not being my biological kid, he sure acted a lot like me.

Still, I understood the real reason why he challenged me every now and then. He needed to know where he stood, whether or not the lines had been redrawn.

I had done the same thing with my father. I'd challenged his word and the rules of his house even more so than Ryan. "Do as I say, not as I do." That saying was my father's favorite, only to be eclipsed by, "So long as I'm putting clothes on your back, food on your plate, and a roof over your head, you will obey my rules."

The only difference between me and my father is that he used a belt for reinforcement. I hadn't needed to resort to the same treatment with Ryan. I hoped I would never have to, but I wouldn't hesitate if I felt it was merited. Thus far, I had made it clear to Ryan and Lucy that there was only one law in our house. Me.

"Will we still go to school? What about my training?" Ryan asked.

"I think a few days off won't hurt either of you."

"Yeah!" Lucy pumped a fist. "Let's go to Disneyland!"

"How about the pool downstairs instead?"

"To the pool!"

"But Master Wen is counting on my help with the others," Ryan whined.

"When everything calms down, then Master Wen can have you back. And anyway, I'm betting a lot of parents will have their kids take the next couple of days off. It wouldn't surprise me if the dojo closes for a bit."

I left them and returned to the lobby. I was surprised to see Reilly standing there with Kang.

"Agent Kang filled me in," Reilly said. "Do you want me to station some men here?"

"Thanks, but I think they'll be fine."

"How are they doing?" he asked.

"They're surviving. What are you doing here?"

"I just got done strategizing with the police chief when Agent Kang called me. Thought I'd stop by."

"What's the latest?" I asked.

"SFPD and the sheriff's department have the city on lockdown. The bridges and major highways have roadblocks in place. The bay is also being heavily patrolled. This guy won't get far for much longer, especially if he's on foot. It's only a matter of time before he's flushed out."

"Has anyone notified Agent House?" I asked. "Everyone who's connected is a potential target, and she's involved."

"She's aware," Reilly answered. "I sent a couple of extra agents to help secure the command center. The Port of Oakland is also on alert. Customs and Border Protection folks are handling security concerns there. What about your place?"

"We had Hansen and Pratt head over there," I said.

"Any other place we should be surveying?"

We both shook our heads.

"The lawyer's death is strange." Reilly rested his hands on his waist. "It could be coincidence, but we'll see what the medical examiner comes back with. I put a call in to have Green handle that one. I want to make sure the lawyer isn't connected. If he is, then our guy changed up his MO."

"I just wish I knew where Xiaolian was," I said. "I firmly believe she's always had the answers to this puzzle."

"Forget about her for the moment. Right now our priority is finding the psycho who gunned down nineteen innocent people today. The two of you need to figure out his next move. I have a nasty feeling this guy isn't done."

"I understand what you're saying, but Xiaolian is the key to everything. She's an integral piece of this investigation. It's all connected."

"Abby, we can't lose another person to this guy. We need to take him out. Only then can we refocus our efforts back on Suitcase Girl. Am I clear here?"

I nodded.

"Listen, the mayor is holding another press conference, and he's requested the heads of law enforcement be present. I know, it's a waste of my time, but people are afraid."

"They should be. Because the only ones who can identify this guy are dead," I said.

"Killers like him are your specialty, Abby. Find him."

Just as Reilly spun on his heels, his cell phone rang.

"Reilly speaking... What happened? Jesus Christ! Do not pursue. I'm ordering you to stand down until backup arrives."

"What?" Kang and I asked in unison.

"The shooter showed up at your home. Pratt's down. Hansen's wounded."

CHAPTER FORTY-EIGHT

HANSEN TIGHTENED his belt around his left arm, just above the elbow. The bullet had passed clean through. Pratt hadn't been so lucky. Shot in the face at point-blank range, he had dropped like a discarded marionette.

When they arrived at Abby's home, the two agents had decided to conduct a walk around the property. As they emerged from the side of the house, they saw the outline of a man standing on the sidewalk. He appeared to be carrying two bags of groceries. The sun had already set, and the only street lamps were posted at the opposite ends of Pfeifer Street, where it intersected with Stockton and Grant. It was darker outside Abby's home.

They approached the man to inquire if he needed any help. Pratt led the way, identifying himself as an FBI agent. That was when the man fired the first shot.

Hansen had just enough time to draw his weapon and return fire while running back around a nearby car. The exchange was brief, but by the time Hansen peeked back over the hood of the vehicle, the shooter had disappeared. He checked on Pratt and confirmed his initial suspicion before calling Reilly. He'd then ignored the order to stand down and went looking for the guy who tried to kill him.

Where did you go, asshole?

Hansen looked up and down the street and figured the guy had reversed course and headed away from the house. He moved forward slowly along the sidewalk, slightly crouched and favoring his arm.

Sirens screamed in the distance. Soon a flurry of red and blue lights would swarm down on his position. Hansen knew a perimeter would be set up in an effort to contain this guy. And that frightened him the most.

The area was purely residential. It was a weeknight, and families were home. Any one of these dwellings could end up as that son-of-a-bitch's last stand. A loose cannon in the corner had no other option but to keep firing.

Clearly this guy had no fear. Death wasn't a deterrent. He had fired on an FBI agent without so much as giving it any thought. Not the kind of guy who surrendered.

Hansen noticed the throbbing in his arm had worsened. Until that point, just the thumping in his chest kept time. His breaths were forceful but not from overexertion. His neck was slick, his eyes jittery, and his trigger finger jumpy.

A lady opened the front door of her home, and Hansen told her to get back inside and lock herself in. He continued down the street, methodically searching, anticipating.

Is that movement?

He turned quickly, pointing his handgun at a tall hedge separating two properties.

I heard something.

He spun around. His eyes searched the low brush across the street.

Come on, Hansen. Pull it together.

His eyes focused back on the street ahead. He stood exactly in the middle of Pfeifer Street. It was also the darkest area. Hansen worked to bring his breathing under control. Each breath sounded like a typhoon blowing.

Surely he had painted himself as a target.

Surely the sights on the shooter's gun were targeting him.

Surely his time had also come.

But Hansen pushed forward. His partner had been gunned down only minutes ago. He had to avenge his death. He couldn't allow him to become another statistic. He had to find this guy. He had to be the one to put an end to this man's reign of terror.

As far as Hansen was concerned, he had no intention of allowing the justice system to play its course. He took on the role of judge and jury that night. And the Glock in his hand was his mallet.

He walked past the tall hedge he had targeted earlier, convinced he was clearing the street as best as he could with each step.

Click.

He was so wrong.

Covering the distance from the hotel to my home was about a six-minute drive, if you drove like I did with a siren screaming, lights flashing, and the accelerator pedal pinned beneath a shoe.

Kang gripped his armrest. "Sheesh, Abby. I think we caught air off that last hill."

He was probably right, but I had brought Hansen and Pratt in on my investigation. They made up my team. I had already failed one of them.

We sped north on Stockton Avenue, barreling through each intersection. Through my rearview mirror, I could see that Reilly was keeping up with us. He had jumped into his SUV and followed me out of the hotel.

The next right was Pfeiffer. I waited until the last possible moment to ease off the gas as I hooked the wheel to the right. The tires screeched as they gripped the pavement, forcing the vehicle to hug the corner. I hit the switch for the high beams and lit the street.

"There!" I shouted.

"I see them." Kang had already drawn his weapon and unfastened his seatbelt.

Ahead of us were two men standing on the sidewalk. One man held a gun against the back of the other's head. I knew Hansen's body posture. There was no mistaking, even at forty yards away, he wasn't the one pointing the weapon.

I slammed my foot down on the brake pedal, and the car came to a quick stop. Both of our doors flew open, and we stepped out, careful to remain behind our metal shields. I heard Reilly's SUV come to halt behind us, his door opening as well.

From our position, we were about fifteen yards away, and the headlights of my vehicle acted like spotlights on a deadly stage.

The shooter looked directly at us. He was Asian, and his clothing fit the description: jeans and a fashionable, long-sleeve button-down. He didn't appear injured, nor did he look like a crazed killer. In fact, he had a calm demeanor.

"Drop the gun!" Kang shouted.

I stared into the man's dark eyes. They were cold, without heart.

"Drop it. Now!" Kang continued with his commands.

A smile formed on the shooter's face.

It was then I realized this would only end one way.

I fired.

So did the shooter.

CHAPTER FORTY-NINE

One man lay face down, the other was on his knees. Kang and I moved forward, weapons still drawn and trained.

"Hansen!" I called out. He didn't answer.

Kang moved to secure the shooter. Reilly was a few steps behind both of us.

I knelt next to Hansen when I reached him. He was shivering and still had a tight grip on his weapon.

"Let's put this down for now," I said as I carefully eased the handgun from his grip. "Everything's under control now."

He looked at me with glassy eyes and tried to speak, but no words came out of his slack jaw. And then he began sobbing. He choked on his breath as tears formed in his eyes before trailing along the sides of his face.

"It's okay." I looked at his arm and adjusted the belt before reaching around and feeling the back of his head. The shooter's bullet had completely missed. "You're fine. You're alive with us here. We got you."

"If you hadn't fired, I—"

"But I did, and you're still here. That's all that matters.

Come on. Stand up." I holstered my weapon and then helped him to his feet. "I want you to wait in the car until a paramedic can look you over."

Hansen slowed as we passed the shooter. Kang was busy checking for a pulse. He didn't have to—the hole in the shooter's head said it all.

I nudged Hansen to keep him moving forward. "Nothing to see here. Let's keep walking."

Of all the newbie agents, Hansen had always stood out to me. He was a go-getter, never afraid to help out and get his hands dirty, and always eager to learn. I'd really had high hopes for him.

But the man I walked next to that night was someone else.

I put Hansen into the front seat of my vehicle. He was still shaking, and his eyes looked right through me.

"Where is Pratt's body?" I asked.

He didn't answer, and his foggy gaze fell to his lap. I lifted his chin and turned his head so his eyes were looking straight into mine. There was nothing there. Just nothing.

I closed the door and went looking for Pratt. Reilly had already found him farther down the street, on the sidewalk outside my home. From the look on Reilly's face, the slight chance that Pratt might still be breathing faded away. The cavalry had come too late.

If you ask me, we lost two agents that night. Even though the shooter's bullet missed the back of Hansen's head by millimeters and he survived, I knew deep down that the chances of him coming back from that were low. That brush with death had shaken him like nothing else.

"How's Agent Hansen?" Reilly asked.

"Aside from the GSW in his left arm, he's alive but..."

Reilly nodded that he understood me. "How did you know the guy would pull the trigger?"

"His eyes. We had him cornered, and he knew that."

"You saved Hansen." Reilly motioned with his head to my vehicle.

"Did I? Did you see him?"

"Give the guy a chance to recover. Some time off and counseling could bring him back."

A load of BS was passing over Reilly's lips. He knew it. I knew it. But that was what supervisors were supposed to say, right?

As first responders filled the street, my neighbors began appearing on their porches and front yards. I couldn't blame them. It wasn't often a shootout took place outside their front doors. I avoided making eye contact with any of them. *I wonder how many of them saw me shoot that man dead.* The media had already turned up. My neighbors could turn on their televisions and receive their briefing that way.

Kang was standing near the shooter's body when I caught up with him. He inquired about Hansen, and I told him the same thing I'd told Reilly, but I could tell Kang knew what was up. He'd heard Hansen sobbing.

"Any idea who the shooter is?" I asked.

"He has no ID. We'll have to print him and see if we get a hit."

I knelt down and lifted the cover that had been placed over the body. I removed my flashlight from the holder on my belt and lit his face for a better look. "You think he's a local or someone sent from China?"

"Hard to say." Kang knelt down next to me. "Not much time has passed since Xiaolian was found. What, like a week? He could have been dispatched from overseas, or he could be a local answering to someone back in the motherland."

"My gut tells me he isn't from here. I also don't see any tattoos that would associate him with any of the large Triad factions in town. That tells me he doesn't work for anyone in particular. He's a contract killer for hire."

"Violent and ruthless way of working too," Kang added.

"If he is from China, his clothing suggests he's from a large city: Beijing, Shanghai, or Hong Kong."

"Or Taiwan, since that's where the ship came from." Kang started checking the clothing tags. "Prada shirt and Guess jeans."

He removed one of the shoes and looked at the label inside before showing it to me. It was a no-name brand. Did it mean anything? Maybe. Finding where the brand was manufactured and sold might pinpoint his home.

"Anything?" Reilly asked as he came up behind us.

I stood. "Nothing to identify him right away. No visible gang tattoos. He doesn't seem local. We'll run his prints through our database and circulate his picture. Hopefully something will come out of that and lead us to the person who hired him."

"If he turns out to be a Chinese national, he's not our problem anymore. The DOJ can run with it, which we know they can't be bothered with, since this doesn't really scream 'national security threat.' The way the powers-that-be will see this playing out is that we caught the mass murderer. The media will call for answers on who he is and why he did this, and we're to say that we're looking into it but it's possible he's working alone."

"That's bullshit," I said.

"I know, Abby, but if he is a Chinese national, it's out of our jurisdiction. As far as the FBI is concerned, we did our part of the job. We caught the guy responsible for killing twenty people today and maybe more."

Reilly was right. Also, we couldn't be sure of why the shooter turned up at my home. Was he after Xiaolian or my family? Either way, until I saw her dead body, I wanted to believe she was still alive.

While her disappearance puzzled me, her existence perplexed me even more. How on earth could a little girl hold the answers to so many questions running through my mind? The most troubling of them all and the one that bothered me the most—why did we look so much alike? Were we meant to find each other?

CHAPTER FIFTY

THE MAN SAT on the bed nearest the television. He had the sound level turned low, barely audible, as he watched the media coverage of the hunt. They were reporting that the police had shot the person responsible but it wasn't official as of yet.

The water to the shower turned off, and he continued to watch, hand ready with the remote. The lock on the bathroom door clicked, and he pressed the off button, but not quick enough. It took a couple of attempts before the TV shut off.

"What's happening?" Xiaolian asked as she exited the bathroom, her eyes locked on the television.

"It's nothing."

"There were a lot of police. Are they looking for me?"

"Why don't you sit down and just rest."

"I want to know what will happen to me now."

"For the time being, you will remain with me."

"But why can't I go back to Abby's house? I don't understand. If you aren't here to take me back, then why do I have to stay with you?"

"It's for your safety."

"You keep saying that, but you won't tell me what you're keeping me safe from."

The man sighed loudly. "You're right. You should know."

He switched the television back on and let her watch the newscast.

"That's Abby's street. I recognize it," Xiaolian said.

The news media continued to report live on the capture of a killer. He didn't bother to prep her or fill in the details. He just allowed her to soak it all in.

After about ten minutes or so of watching, she turned to him. "The others from the boat, they're all dead?"

"I'm afraid so."

"Why were they killed?"

"Good question. I don't know why."

Just then cameras were panning across the crime scene, and Agent Kane walked by.

"There's Abby." She pointed at the television set. "Did she catch the killer?"

"I believe she was involved."

"Then it's safe."

"It's not confirmed."

"Well, if they confirm it, I can go back to Abby's house."

He didn't answer her. He didn't even look at her, just kept staring at the television. He wasn't sure what his next move should be. He'd been lucky to get Xiaolian out of the house when he had. If he hadn't, she might be dead, and then all of their work, all the planning, the risks, and the lives lost would be for naught.

And in all honesty, he wasn't the deciding factor. He himself followed orders.

"I can't go back to her, can I?" she asked, a bit more force-fully this time.

"I don't know. It's not up to me. You know that. Let me ask you something—do you know why Abby allowed you to stay with her?"

Xiaolian thought for a moment before answering. "I don't know."

"She needed answers, and you could provide them."

"But maybe she likes me. Maybe she'll want to keep me even if she has her answers."

He leaned forward, rested his forearms on his thighs, and lowered his head. He didn't know what to tell her.

"They're speaking again," she said, pointing at the television.

He looked up. A reporter was interviewing a man with the FBI. The screen caption read "Special Agent in Charge Scott Reilly."

"At approximately ten after nine, I received a call from Agent Oliver Hansen. He and Agent Patrick Pratt had stopped a man to question him. This person then opened fire, and Agent Pratt was shot dead. Agent Hansen was also wounded. Despite his injury, he gave chase to the suspect. I and two other federal agents arrived to find the killer with his gun drawn and targeting Agent Hansen. We opened fire, shooting that person dead."

"I think the questions that are on everyone's one mind tonight is: who is this man and what prompted him to kill all these innocent people?" a reporter said.

"Those are questions we're working to find answers to."

The reporter continued with her line of questioning. "What about the victims? Was there any connection between them or was this all completely random and a case of being in the wrong place at the wrong time?"

"Again, that's something we're working on. We've yet to identify all of the victims."

"It's our understanding that some of the victims found at the women's shelter were in fact women who were trafficked into this country illegally and forced to work as underage prostitutes."

"I'm sorry, but that's not something I can yet comment on as we're still investigating."

"Is it not true that these women, or really, teenagers, were in fact rescued, and that's why they were in the shelter in the first place?"

"It is."

"So perhaps the people responsible for trafficking them came after these girls to keep them from talking."

"Like I said earlier, we're investigating, and as soon as we know more, we'll report on it. That's all for now."

The reporter turned to the camera. "You heard it here first on KTVU. The man responsible for the worst mass shooting to affect the Bay Area has been killed. Twenty people were shot dead today, and as it stands, only a handful have been identified." The reporter adjusted her earpiece. "Just a minute, I'm receiving word that we have confirmation on some of the victims at the shelter."

Images of three victims then filled the screen as the reporter went on to say they were all employees of the shelter.

"I know that lady," Xiaolian said as a picture of Massey, the director of the shelter, appeared on the screen. "She was very nice to me."

While watching, the man wondered if it was really over.

Had the police really caught the person responsible? Was it safe to go on with their plan?

After another twenty minutes passed, the reporter claimed they had more breaking news. The police had released a picture of the shooter. Seconds later, the face of an Asian male appeared.

The doctor leaned forward, looking closely at him. He quickly snapped a photo with his phone so he could study it further. As the reporter went on to say that this was the man responsible for the deaths that day, he peered at the photo.

Why does he look familiar?

He wracked his brain, searching for information. And then it dawned on him. The police had indeed caught the man responsible, only they hadn't caught the other one.

"Is it finally over?" the girl asked.

He looked over at her and shook his head. "I don't think it'll ever be over."

CHAPTER FIFTY-ONE

It was late and CSI was still processing the crime scene outside my house. I offered to give Kang a lift back to the office so he could retrieve his car, but instead he just had me drop him off at his place. He didn't live very far from me, just on the other side of Russian Hill.

"I'm beat. I just want to go home, take a shower, and crawl into bed."

"That makes two of us," I said.

"Are you bringing everyone back to the house?"

One of the lab techs walked by us as we got into my vehicle.

"I think I'll keep them at the hotel for now. I don't want them seeing any of this."

"Probably already saw it on the news."

"You're right. And I'm sure every kid in school will bring it up to them."

"It's unavoidable." Kang secured his seatbelt.

During the drive, we fell silent for a few minutes, though my thoughts were still racing. "We're still nowhere with Xiaolian," I said, breaking the silence.

"I know," Kang said. "Anyone who we might have wanted to question is dead."

"I think that was the point. In the end, they won and we lost."

"I guess you could look at it that way. Maybe this 'they' are the ones who took Xiaolian."

"I wonder if 'they' should have gotten her from the very beginning," I said.

"What do you mean?" he asked.

"Maybe Chow was supposed to deliver her to someone and not to our offices—somehow instructions got mixed up or someone gave him the wrong information."

"And all of what happened today was simply the righting of the wrong?"

"I know I'm reaching, but I'm just trying to figure out Xiaolian's role in all of this. And yes, I do believe she's the center of it all."

"I'm with you on that." Kang let out a soft breath. "The problem is everything we're discussing right now is just theory. It's us trying to find a rationale, and the truth is we could be one-hundred-percent wrong."

"I know. We may be so far off of the mark it's laughable."

I came to a stop outside of Kang's Victorian. He lived alone. His girlfriend, now ex, had moved out a while ago, at least a year.

"Let's not get wound up about it right now," he said as he opened his door. "We've both had a long day. We'll get a good night's sleep and come at this fresh in the morning."

"Sounds good."

I waited until he reached his front door and went inside before driving off. Kang was a good guy. Who would have thought when we first met in Chinatown that we would end up being partners? Not I, that was for sure. My first impression of him had been dismal. Luckily he recovered well.

I got back to the hotel a little after midnight. There was a small living room area with two couches. Ryan had passed out on one, with the TV still on—a martial arts movie. I switched it off and then checked the bedroom. Lucy and Po Po were asleep on the bed.

I took a quick shower and then lay down on the couch opposite Ryan. I had just closed my eyes when I heard him say my name.

"Abby?"

"Yes."

"Will the agent who got shot be okay?"

"He will. Why do you ask?"

"It makes me sad that he got hurt."

"It makes me sad too."

"It could have been you who got shot."

I thought about my answer for moment as I lay there in the dark. I decided honesty was in order. "You're right. It could have been me, but what you need to know is that I will always do everything in my power to ensure that I don't get hurt."

"But you can't always control everything."

"That's true. Keeping others, including you, your sister, and Po Po safe from bad guys can be dangerous."

"Someone's gotta do it."

I chuckled at his honesty. "You're right."

"You know what? I like helping people too. Today at school I helped a boy who was being bullied."

"What happened?" I turned over to my side so I was facing Ryan.

"A kid from a higher class was picking on this smaller kid. I don't know all of the background, but the smaller kid wasn't trying to fight him. He just wanted to be left alone, but the bigger kid kept pushing him."

"So what did you do?"

"I told the bigger kid to leave him alone."

"And then what?"

"He told me to f-off?"

"What? Tell me this kid's name. I'll call his mother and—"

"Don't worry, Abby. I handled it."

"Oh, did you? And exactly how did you *handle* it?"

"Let's just say when he told me he would knock me out, he didn't make good on his promise."

"Where were all the teachers?"

"We were in the boys' bathroom, but I'm not telling you this because of the fight. What I'm trying to say is, even though this other kid was bigger than me, I knew the smaller kid couldn't protect himself. I at least know martial arts, so I had a shot. So I did what you do—I protected him from the bad guy."

I couldn't have been any prouder of Ryan at that moment, and I told him so before telling him to go to back to bed. For the first time since I'd been involved in my children's lives, I felt like I had truly done something right as a mom, something that had a positive effect.

CHAPTER FIFTY-TWO

WITH THE CITY's mass murderer dead, I saw no reason to keep the kids home from school and broke the news to them while we were having breakfast in the suite.

"Awww, man. Why so fast?" Lucy stabbed her waffles with her fork. "I haven't even had a chance to unwind."

"Why do you need to unwind?" I asked.

"I have a lot on my mind. Everyday it's nonstop."

I started to laugh.

"I'm serious," she said.

And I could see that she was, but the thought of an eight-year-old complaining about her daily decisions... well, it was a bit much.

"Okay, okay. So you have a lot on your mind. Guess what? It gets worse as you age."

"Really? This is what I have to look forward to? More decisions? Oh my goodness."

Not long ago, Lucy had discovered Shirley Temple during a marathon showing on one of the cable channels and began channeling the curly-haired singer. 'Oh my goodness' had fast become her favorite saying. She also started talking more while resting her hands on her hips. She even asked me if she could get a perm. Ryan and I had made a bet on how long this phase would last. I had it at under month, he had it at over.

We were closing in on a month. Ryan sat across the table from me and bounced his eyebrows at me twice and then pointed to his watch. He would win this bet and get his wish. Ever since he heard of the intern program run by the FBI for teenagers, he'd bugged me to let him sign up when he was of age.

I was on the fence with his interest in law enforcement. I knew how dangerous and unforgiving the job could be—it was not something I wanted for him. I preferred something safe and stable, like a dentist or a banker or even a developer like his father. But after his revelation the night before, maybe he was suited for a career in law enforcement. There are many types of jobs in that industry that didn't involve getting shot at by the bad guys. He certainly had the smarts to be an analyst or maybe work as a crime scene investigator.

After we checked out of the hotel, I dropped the kids off at school and then drove Po Po home. I changed into fresh clothing and headed into the office.

I bumped into Kang in the lobby. "Howdy, pardner."

"Morning," he said. He carried a brown paper bag in one hand. "Sleep okay last night?"

"Slept fine. Could have slept longer. What's in the bag?" I asked, knowing full well it was something edible.

"Bao."

He reached into the bag and removed a fluffy, white bun and handed it to me. I quickly took a bite. The warm, sweet bun was stuffed with seasoned braised pork.

"Mmmm."

As we rode the elevator up to our floor, we bit, chewed, and swallowed while continually grunting like a couple of cavemen in suits enjoying the spoils of a hunt.

We exited the elevator onto a floor that was usually flowing with a buzz and a whole lot of hustle from agents working their investigations. That morning it was different. Everyone had heard about Pratt's death, and it was a reminder that we were vulnerable and could end up on the losing end.

Kang's one-year anniversary with the Bureau was coming up. Probably not the best time to throw a celebratory dinner with the agents we worked closely with. Hansen and Pratt were two of them. Still, I didn't want to forget about it. It was a big deal for Kang to leave the SFPD, and I wanted him to feel like he'd made the right choice. Sure, I talked his ear off about how wonderful it would be to work with *moi*, his favorite agent, but I knew deep down inside it wasn't a deciding factor. Kang made his own decisions. He never did tell me what had convinced him to do it. He just said he'd given it some thought and decided it was a good move.

If I don't bring it up now, the day will come and go. "So I was thinking..."

"I'm not interested in having a celebratory dinner for my one-year anniversary with the Bureau," he said.

"What makes you think I was talking about that? I just said I was thinking."

"I know you, Abby. Look, I appreciate the thought, but now's not the time." He made a stinky face as he held both palms up.

"It's the perfect time. This is about you, not about what happened last night. It was unfortunate and we all feel badly, but it shouldn't take away from you and your productive year here. Plus we need to eat anyway."

"I don't know, Abby."

"Okay, how about dinner at my place? I'll invite House and Reilly, that's it. We'll keep it small and informal. We'll grill in the backyard. In fact, we'll make it potluck. You can make your famous Japanese-style potato salad."

Kang mulled my proposition for a moment or so. "Okay, that's sounds fine. Thanks, partner."

"No problem, man-who-always-feeds-me-tasty-food." I then reached into the bag and grabbed another bao. "When you worked with Sokolov, did you feed him as well?"

Kang shrugged. "Sometimes. He really likes his Russian food. It's specific, and you either have to make it yourself or buy something from one of the Russian delis in the Inner Richmond."

"Should we ask him and Bennie to join us? It's not a problem."

"Why not? He likes meat."

"Okay, it's settled. This weekend at my house."

CHAPTER FIFTY-THREE

OVER THE COURSE of the next two days, we got absolutely nowhere with our investigation into Xiaolian's disappearance. She had vanished just as mysteriously as she had appeared. We even questioned Medina and Watts again about the shipments at the port, but they both confirmed it was always Chow and his crew that showed up. They never saw anyone else.

The only interesting thing to pop up was learning the cause of death of Yu, the lawyer. Dr. Green had moved pretty fast on the autopsy of the body. Kang had decided not to tag along, so I went over to his office by myself.

The Office of the Medical Examiner was located on Bryant Street, tucked away inside the Office of Justice. Over the years, I had made many trips there and had gotten to know Green fairly well. During that time, he developed a schoolboy crush on me. I did use it to my advantage at times when I needed something from him, I had to admit. But mostly I tried to treat the gentle doctor as a colleague and a friend.

I waited in a sanitized space they called a waiting room. Cold and medical described it best. Green appeared through double swinging doors wearing a white lab coat that always looked a size too large for him—his hands disappeared into the sleeves.

He still wore the small Ben Franklin spectacles that rested on the bump of his nose; bushy eyebrows lived above them and were equally matched by his unkempt hair.

Underneath the unbuttoned coat, he wore one of his many colorful T-shirts. That day he wore a light-blue shirt with a quote on the front: "If it's yellow, let it mellow. If it's brown, flush it down."

"So nice to see you, Abby," he said in a soft voice.

He opened his arms and went in for the hug. I was faster and extended my arm for a handshake. Green hugged longer than most, and he and I were about the same height, so a friendly embrace between us looked more than what it really was. There were others in the waiting room that day, and I felt I needed to keep our greeting professional.

"I see you have yourself a new earring," I said. He always wore a tiny diamond stud. That day a silver and turquoise piece dangled from his earlobe.

"Yes, a present from my niece. She recently took a jewelry-making class, and I'm the lucky recipient of one of her works of art."

"It suits you just fine. Lucky you."

"Come on." He motioned toward the double doors. "Do you know the difference between a corpse and a bore? They're both stiffs." Green chuckled at his own joke while pushing one of the doors open.

The scent of patchouli wafted off of Green as I followed him down a long corridor. The fluorescent lighting above buzzed louder than usual, but at least the flickering had been curbed since my last visit.

He stopped outside a familiar green door. The room inside was where Green performed all of his autopsies. From what I understood, only he used it. The other medical examiners used one of the other autopsy rooms.

Green was a bit eccentric, but he was the best in the city, perhaps even the country. He loved investigating the dead. "It's just me and that person having a one-on-one conversation about what happened," he had once mentioned to me.

Inside were four stainless steel tables surrounded by gutters. Yu's body was the only one in the room and lay under a gray sheet on the table farthest from the door.

"Slow day, huh?" I said.

"Dead slow." Green's smile grew, and his shoulders bounced a little.

He removed the sheet and revealed Yu's naked body. The man had a pleasant look on his face, as if he had died peacefully. A Y incision had been made lengthwise down the middle of his torso and had yet to be stapled shut.

"Care to take a guess?" Green asked.

"Heart attack?"

"You're partially right."

"How can I be partially right?"

"He did suffer a massive heart attack, and that's what ultimately killed him, but the real culprit is what caused the heart attack."

"Huh?"

"Have you ever heard of potassium chloride?"

"I know you get potassium from eating bananas."

"You're right. Potassium chloride is made up of potassium

and chlorine, and both are compounds naturally found in the human body. But high levels of potassium can cause tachycardia, which is a fast heart rate. This can lead to a heart attack."

"So when the potassium chloride breaks down, it leaves no trace, and the result is what seems to be a naturally occurring heart attack, right?"

"Very good." Green smiled as he nodded.

"So how can you be sure this was the cause?"

Green snapped on latex gloves before using a cavity spreader to pry Yu's chest apart. Once open, he reached inside and lifted up Yu's heart so we were looking at its backside. "You see how this area is blackish in color?"

"Yeah..."

"A high concentration of potassium chloride can cause discoloring to the heart."

"So what did he do, eat twenty bananas really quickly?"

"Injection would be the likely method. However, I found no defensive wounds or bruising on his forearms, also no foreign DNA was found under his nails to suggest he fought someone off."

"So are you saying he committed suicide?"

Green moved around to Yu's feet. He took his left foot and lifted it slightly. "Look right here. See that hole? That's where he injected himself. I'm guessing if you go back and search that house again, you'll likely find a syringe somewhere."

"Everyone else connected was executed. Why Yu would commit suicide is a bit baffling. Unless he was the man responsible for ordering the hits."

"You're surmising that he ordered the hits then killed himself to close up the loose end?"

I folded my arms across my chest. "I know, seems a little

fantastical, but people like this are. Well, now that we know he killed himself—"

"The question is whether it was by force or voluntarily." Green removed the gloves and tossed them into a nearby trash bin.

"Yes, but you already said that you found no signs to indicate he was under any physical duress."

"True, but the thing is... this is not a pleasant way to die. The pain he would have experienced in his chest is incomprehensible, akin to setting oneself on fire, if I had to put it in terms to grasp. This man had to have had a very good reason to want to die this way."

CHAPTER FIFTY-FOUR

AFTER MY MEETING WITH GREEN, I made my way back to the office. Kang sat at his desk, staring at his computer.

"Struggling to craft that perfect email response?" I asked as I approached.

"Not everyone is a master zinger like you. How did it go?"

"There's been no shedding of the light."

"Huh?"

"Come on." I motioned for him to follow me. "Let's head into Reilly's office so I only have to tell this story once."

I knocked on the door to the boss's office and poked my head inside. "Gotta minute?"

Reilly closed a file folder and set it aside. "Yeah, come in, guys."

"Green finished the autopsy. It's his opinion that the lawyer committed suicide."

"Is there a connection to our shooter?"

"Nothing decisive, but there's something about the suicide that gave me pause. Green believes Yu injected himself with potassium chloride. High concentrations of it can trigger a massive heart attack."

"Abby, I'm not getting the importance of this meeting. So Yu killed himself and there's no connection to our shooter." Reilly shrugged, acting annoyed.

"I think Yu is connected and not just by the fact that he was Chow's lawyer."

"So you think he's the one who orchestrated this massacre and then committed suicide because he was sure all tracks would lead back to his doorstep?"

Wow, someone's sick of eating bran for breakfast.

"Maybe, but that's just it. I'm not sure what the connection is or what his role was, but representing Chow and his crew with no other clients to speak of and then suddenly committing suicide... well, it's suspect."

Reilly looked over at Kang. "You seem awfully quiet."

"I think Abby's got a point, and it's worth looking into."

"Fine. Chase your hunch," Reilly said as he gestured for us to leave his office.

Kang buried his hands into his pants pockets as we headed back to our desks. "Is that all Green said?"

"In a nutshell. Green mentioned if we could find the syringe Yu used to inject himself, he could examine it and possibly have more answers."

"CSI already combed the place. A needle wasn't listed on the evidence report."

"Maybe they missed it."

We were in the middle of gathering our items when Reilly stuck his head out of his office and called us back in.

Now what?

When we returned to his office, Reilly was sitting behind his desk and standing next to him was a thin man wearing a white lab coat with a smile on his face.

"Have a seat, guys. This is Agent Richard Vasquez."

"Wow, you really do look alike," Vasquez commented. "I'm sorry, Agent Kane. We've never met in person, but I know you through email. Well, I've seen your name. Anyway, I heard about the connection with the little girl, but I didn't expect it to be so... well, you must hear this from everyone—"

"Agent Vasquez. Why don't you get to the point," Reilly pushed.

"Yes, of course." Vasquez chuckled nervously. "A little background. I'm the one who pulled the DNA from the suitcase and matched it to Chow's."

"I appreciate that. It was helpful," I said.

Vasquez continued to smile. In fact he hadn't stopped since we entered Reilly's office.

"Well, I also did something else with, um, with the girl's DNA that wasn't asked of me, but my mind has a way of wandering. Often it's helpful because it can lead to new discoveries, which I just happened to have stumbled across."

"You identified Xiaolian?"

"Who?"

"That's what we're calling Suitcase Girl," I clarified.

"Oh, okay. Yeah makes sense. It's a nicer name than the other. Okay, anyway... I, ah, sort of identified her."

"Define 'sort of,'" I said as I crossed one leg over the other.

"I'll just come out and say it. I tested Xiaolian's DNA with your DNA."

My mouth fell slack. "Why on earth would you do that?"

"Like I said earlier, sometimes my mind wanders and I go

off in directions that weren't necessarily required. And we had your DNA samples on file. Anyway, I did the test."

"And..." The tone of my voice clearly displayed my irritation.

"I probably should have told you before I did it, but—"

"Agent Vazquez, are you about to imply that you discovered the girl and I are related? Because if that's where this conversation is heading, then I'm sorry to burst your bubble."

"No, that's just it. I'm not trying to say that the two of you are related. It's more than that. She's you."

CHAPTER FIFTY-FIVE

For the first time since I laid eyes on Vasquez, his nervous smile faltered and I realized he was dead serious about whatever nonsense he was talking about.

"Like I said earlier, if you're implying that Xiaolian is my daughter... well, you should know that I'm aware of what pregnancy is and what it looks like and I would have known if I had given birth to a child. I'm not one of those people who suddenly pops a kid out in a bathroom stall, thinking all along the bulging stomach was nothing more than bad gas." I looked at Kang. "Tell me you're not buying this load of bull."

He offered a half-hearted shrug.

"Am I the only one who finds this claim preposterous?"

"Agent Kane I realize what I'm saying may be hard to grasp, but if you allow me to explain, I can help you to understand."

I folded my arms across my chest. "I'm waiting."

"I'm not saying she's your daughter. I'm saying she's you."

He opened his laptop and set it on the desk in front of me. "You have an 80% DNA match with the girl. Only 50% is needed to match a child with a parent. Trust me, I redid the test over and over just to be sure."

"Abby, maybe you have a younger sister your parents didn't tell you about," Kang said.

"I doubt it. I would know. I'm an only child."

"That's not what I'm inferring either," Vasquez said. "She's not a sibling. I also found two other sources of DNA that don't match yours."

"How can that be?"

"It's called three-parenting. It's when the DNA of a third person is introduced into another egg."

Vasquez must have noticed my eye roll.

"I'm serious, Agent Kane. This is a real procedure that exists, though what I'm seeing here is much more advanced than what's been published thus far in scientific journals. It's astonishing."

"Wait. Just so I'm clear. You're saying my DNA was intro-duced into some stranger's egg and then fertilized."

Vasquez nodded. "I'll admit, this isn't my field, but I've read about three-parenting. It's been used successfully to change the DNA makeup of a child, mostly to edit out a disease if one parent has a history of it."

"Is this like the designer genes, where parents can pick the eye color of their children?" Kang asked.

"It is, but it's much more advanced. That's just altering existing DNA. What we have here is entirely new DNA, in this case Agent Kane's, replacing existing DNA. What we're seeing here is light-years ahead. And from what I've learned so far, your DNA was tinkered with to be the dominant one. Really the other two served as hosts—a way to grow the embryo into a healthy baby."

"Are you talking about cloning?" Reilly asked.

"No, it's not cloning either. If it were, the DNA would be one-hundred-percent identical. What we have here, if I had to put it in other words, is more like counterfeiting. Someone created a pretty good replica of you."

"Why on earth would someone want to replicate me? Why would two people who want a baby use my DNA and make it the dominant one? It's like the baby isn't even representative of them. And secondly, is that really even possible?"

"Like I said earlier, I'm not an expert on this work, but I don't think whoever did this wanted to clone you because of the three-parenting. They just wanted a good replica. A way to take whatever traits they liked about you and put that into another person. And to answer your second question, it's a lot easier than you think. All someone would need to do is scrub you."

"Scrub?"

"Take blood, hair, and skin samples."

I could feel a headache creeping up the back of my head. I was flabbergasted by what Vasquez was saying.

"So you're saying someone stole my DNA?"

"This girl is about eleven or twelve. Where were you eleven or twelve years ago?"

"I was living in Hong Kong."

"Were you ever hospitalized during that time, or do you remember being in a position where someone could scrub these samples from you?"

"Well, I was hospitalized once—pneumonia. You think someone took my DNA during that time?"

"I do. It's the only way this girl can exist as she is."

"I can't believe I'm even continuing to have this conversation. What about you guys?" I looked at Kang and then at Reilly. "Are you guys buying this?"

Silence on their end filled the room. Neither man had an answer, or at least weren't willing to give one.

Vasquez continued. "I'm sorry I don't have all the answers. Ideally, we need to bring in an expert, but I would love to run more tests on the girl in the meantime. It's my understanding she's staying with you."

"I forgot to mention the hiccup to him," Reilly said.

"Mention what?"

"Xiaolian is missing," I said. "She was taken from my home."

CHAPTER FIFTY-SIX

Two DAYS LATER, on Saturday, Xiaolian lay on the bed, staring at the popcorn ceiling. The television aired the newscast, but she wasn't really paying attention, as the volume was always kept low or muted.

She already knew the police had captured the man responsible for murdering all those people, and now it seemed like all they were focused on was why he did it. They were always showing his picture. The funny thing was the police had yet to identify the man.

Of course, Xiaolian knew his name was Alonzo Chan thanks to Dr. Jian Lee, the man who had helped orchestrate her escape to the States and from Abby's home.

She was never told why she needed to escape from the facility she used to call home. All she was told was that it was important that she did. She never questioned—not when she was whisked out of her bed in the middle of the night, not when she was told to run through the woods, not when she was told to get into the trunk of a car and be quiet.

For as long as she could remember, no one at the facility

disobeyed the staff. To do so resulted in punishments ranging from the withholding of a meal to solitary confinement to physical exhaustion. And in the most severe cases, disappearing for good, never to be heard from again.

However, there was one thing she did know for sure. Something she had come to remember. It had been made clear to her how important it was that she and Agent Abby Kane find each other. They were destined to meet, as Agent Kane was the answer.

"How much longer must we stay here?" she asked without her eyes leaving the ceiling.

"I'm not sure," said Lee as he sat on the other bed, watching the newscast.

"Why? They've caught the man. It's safe to go back to Abby's home."

"No it's not." He switched off the television.

"I don't understand why you keep information from me. I may be a child, but I don't expect to be treated like one. Am I not the chosen one?"

"You are, and that is why it is even more important that you remain safe. We can't afford to lose you. There is no one at the moment who meets all the requirements to replace you. Trust me, if there were, you would not have been chosen for such an important task."

"You're speaking your mind," she said, finally turning her head in his direction. "We're becoming comfortable with each other."

"And you're becoming your old self again. That mouth of yours serves no positive purpose."

"Is that so? I think you just don't like when I, or any of the others, question you, and yet you seem to forget that questioning is the very trait that makes us great."

Lee didn't respond, but looked away from her instead.

"I'm sorry. I shouldn't be angry with you. I know you're here to help me." She sat up, her legs dangling over the side of the bed. "What will happen to you when this is over?"

"I'm not sure. My job was to ensure your safety. There were many unforeseeable events that took place. We're lucky there were no setbacks, just delays."

"I understand. I have an important job to do."

"Do you truly?"

"Yes, I'm sure."

"Then you know the name they call you, Xiaolian, isn't your real name?"

She nodded.

"Can you tell me what it really is?"

"It's Abby."

He nodded as he allowed his gaze to fall to the forest-green carpeting in the room. A worn path in front of the two beds lightened the color.

"What's wrong?" she asked.

"Everything. I'm beginning to think maybe this was all a big mistake."

"But they caught the bad man."

"They killed one of the two brothers. What you don't understand is that Walter Chan, the other brother, is a dangerous man. He'll keep coming for you until your name is crossed off his list or he's killed."

"Can we tell the police about him? Maybe they can help." Xiaolian's gaze fell to her feet, where she watched them trace circles.

"The only person who can stop him is the person who hired him, and that won't ever happen unless... you return."

"Return?" Xiaolian looked up. "Why would we do that? We haven't come all this way just to go back."

"We never anticipated something like this happening. We're in over our heads. Everyone who has helped you get this far is either dead or in hiding, fearing for their lives."

"If we turn back now, then they've been sacrificed for nothing."

"We didn't know they would send the Chan brothers. It was inconceivable. If we return, this all can end. Perhaps we can make peace and prevent more people from dying."

But, but, but. The words were in her head, but her mouth refused to utter them. She couldn't believe he was contemplating returning. Surely that would only result in unfathomable punishment, the likes of which none had yet seen. Even she knew that was a dumb decision.

"Don't you want to do the right thing?" he asked.

"We are doing the right thing," she blurted.

"Are you okay with more people being hurt?"

"Why is this my decision anyway? I didn't choose this." A forceful breath passed through her pouty lips. Xiaolian couldn't bring herself to look at Lee. She couldn't believe after everything that had happened, he was suggesting they go back. *What a weak man.*

A silence fell upon the room, building a wall between the two as they retreated into their thoughts. If it weren't for the buzzing cell phone on the table, they might have not said another word for the remainder of the night.

The rattling plastic case against the Formica tabletop jolted the man out of his thoughts. Lee crinkled his brow as he watched the phone hum for attention. He looked over at Xiao-lian. "Did you use my phone?"

She said nothing and lay back on the bed.

"I asked you a question."

She lifted her head. "I wanted to see where we were on the map."

"Didn't I tell you never to use it?"

"I don't see what the big deal is. It's not like I called someone."

"I always keep it powered off unless I need to use it. Want to know why? I'll tell you. It prevents someone from tracking us through the phone's GPS signal."

He reached for the phone and answered it.

"Hello?"

Xiaolian stole peeks at him.

"Hello? Hello?"

He quickly disconnected the call and then reached for the black duffle bag he kept near his bed and removed a handgun.

"Why do you have a gun?"

"We're in trouble."

"Who was on the phone?"

"I think he's found us." Lee walked over to the curtained window near the door and peeked outside.

"Is he there?" she asked.

"I don't know," he said, looking back at her. "It's not safe here for you. You must leave, now." He moved away from the window and toward her.

She pointed and gasped, prompting him to turn around. The silhouette of a person, moving slowly, passed by the curtained window.

"He's here," the doctor said in a whisper. He grabbed her

arm. "Come on." He led her to the bathroom. "Can you fit through that window?"

Xiaolian looked at the square window. "I think so."

Lee pried it open and then helped her up onto the toilet.

"But how will you fit?" she asked.

"I won't. You know where we are, right? Can you find your way back to Abby's home?"

"I don't know. Maybe."

He tucked the phone into the back pocket of her jeans. "If you get lost, turn the phone on, use the map to find your bearings, and then turn it back off. Do not leave it on. Understand?"

She looked past him, prompting him to turn around. The silhouette had appeared outside the window again, only this time it had stopped.

"You must hurry."

He placed the handgun down on the sink and then clasped his hands together for her to use it as a step. Up she went. She easily shuffled her head, shoulders, and torso through the window.

"Can you climb down?" he asked.

"Yes."

With her body halfway out the window, she worked to squeeze a leg through, so that she wouldn't fall face first onto the pavement below. Their hotel room was located on the ground level, so there wasn't a drop.

The sound of the doorknob being rattled prompted him to shove the rest of Xiaolian through the window. Her foot caught itself on the windowsill.

"I'm stuck," she said.

Again, the doorknob rattled, louder this time.

Lee grabbed her shoe and angled it downward, then forced it through the window.

Something banged against the front door, shaking it in its frame.

Xiaolian began pulling her other leg through the window as she straddled the bottom of the sill, her torso completely outside.

The banging against the door continued. Each hit louder and much more forceful. Any second, it would crash open. Lee held on to both of Xiaolian's hands as she began lowering herself. One by one she transferred her grip from his hands to the windowsill. No sooner had she done this, the banging stopped.

Lee grabbed the gun and exited the bathroom, closing the door behind him just as a kick sent the door to the room flying open.

Standing in the doorway was a man. The setting sun behind him cast his image as a shadow, but Lee didn't need a spotlight on the person's face to know that Walter Chan had found them.

CHAPTER FIFTY-SEVEN

THAT SATURDAY AFTERNOON we had commenced with the BBQ in my backyard to celebrate Kang's one-year anniversary with the Federal Bureau of Investigation. Everyone showed up: Reilly, House, Sokolov, Bennie, and Dr. Green.

Yes, Green. I had inadvertently mentioned it to him while at his office, and he'd quickly expressed his desire to come, which I found surprising since he and Kang didn't really have the friendliest of relations. That fact didn't seem to bother Green, so I relented and told him he was more than welcome to come over. "I'll bring my famous baked beans," he'd said happily. "Everyone will love it."

And we did. Those beans were damn good.

On the grill, we had ribs, chicken, and sausages. Kang commandeered the grill from the moment he arrived. "Abby, I love grilling. This is not a bother, so leave me be."

Po Po made Kang's favorite dish: Peking noodles. She fixed him a plate while he grilled, as he just couldn't wait. Reilly brought fresh oysters from Tomales Bay, and we shucked and shucked and shucked. Sokolov indulged us with Russian salad and cheese, and his homemade pickled vegetables. Bennie brought tamales he'd made using his mother's recipe. House supplied the dessert—an apple, a blueberry, and a peach pie. No one there would say they left hungry.

By the time the sun had begun to set, most everyone had a stuffed belly. Kang and I were sitting on lounge chairs around a custom fire pit I'd had installed a few months ago. It was the perfect day with loads of laughter and hearty conversation, and with the best company I could ask for.

Kang sipped his beer. "I'll admit, I wasn't expecting Green to turn up, but all in all, I'm having a great time."

"You see? You two *can* get past your jealousies over me."

"Are we bringing this up again? I tell you..."

"Hold that thought. I'll be right back."

The cooler was low on ice, and I had another bag sitting in the freezer in the kitchen. Lucy noticed me heading inside and quickly followed.

"Where are you going, Mommy? Is the party over?"

"No, it's not. I'm just getting more ice."

"Oh good, because I'm having a lot of fun."

Ryan ran right by us.

"Hey, where's the fire?" I shouted.

He stopped at the foot of the steps. "I'm getting my nunchucks. I want to show Uncle Kyle how much I've improved."

"He's not going anywhere anytime soon, so slow down, all right?"

"Okay, okay." He turned and raced up the stairs.

Just as I pulled a bag of ice out of the freezer, the doorbell rang. Lucy, as usual, bolted toward the front door. I was still on edge with the recent killings and called out to her not to open the door, but by the time I had reached the living room, she had already pulled it wide open.

In an instant I froze in step as I recognized the man standing in the doorway. Lucy was wrong when she'd called out that we had another guest. I knew this man, but he was definitely not invited to the BBQ. I simply couldn't believe he was standing there. *Impossible.* And I knew this to be factual because I remember staring into his empty eyes after I'd shot him dead.

But there he was, on my front porch. Alive.

CHAPTER FIFTY-EIGHT

"Lucy!"

No matter how much I forced my legs to move faster, no matter how hard I pumped my arms, it seemed as if I could not reach her. Why was it taking so long? Why was she not heeding my calls to move away from the door? Why did she continue to stand there? There were no logical answers to the series of whys filling my head.

None of this made any sense. How could the killer I'd shot dead be standing on my front porch? And yet there he was.

"Lucy, get away from him!"

She looked back at me, a smile on her face. Didn't she know? Didn't she recognize the man standing before her? Hadn't she seen his picture on the news?

At that moment I realized I was responsible. I had done my best to shield her from the killings, and those efforts were quickly turning into the very thing that endangered her. Had she watched the news, had she seen his picture, had she been aware of the dangers that plagued our city, she would never have opened the door to a stranger.

Instinctively my hand shot to my hip where I always wore my holster. But I knew before my hand reached down that my gun wasn't on me. I never carried it at home. I always kept my weapon in my bedroom upstairs on the second floor.

The thought to turn and run upstairs to retrieve it crossed my mind briefly, but I knew that wouldn't do me any good. His right hand was already sliding up his torso and into the open sport jacket he wore.

No! This can't be happening.

A smirk appeared on his face. He knew I was unarmed. He held the power to decide the events that unfolded in the next few seconds.

As I struggled to close the gap between us, I couldn't keep my eyes off of his hand. I watched it disappear inside his coat briefly before returning to view.

Firmly in his grip I saw the black metal of the handgun's barrel. His hand moved in an arc as he trained his weapon on his target.

It wasn't me.

The barrel of the gun swung around and stopped just above where Lucy stood. His gaze never once left mine as he lowered the gun. I watched him point the weapon straight at her forehead. She was no longer looking at me but at the man in front of her.

What was she thinking? Had her smile disappeared at that point? Did she know of the danger she was in? Was she capable of realizing she had to run?

She's not moving.

She's not screaming.

The worst possible outcome had come to fruition.

She froze.

Kang had shot off his chair the instant he heard Abby scream. He knew her well enough to know that her shouting Lucy's name had nothing to do with disciplining her. There was fear woven throughout it. Something terrible had happened.

"Kyle?" House called out. She had been talking to Reilly.

Kang didn't answer but zeroed in on the door leading into the screened-in porch—a path to the inside of the house. At that moment, he knew deep down inside that every second counted. He couldn't waste a moment explaining. He pulled open the screen door and slipped between a small table and a rattan loveseat, his right hand stretched outward for the door leading into the house.

Unlike Abby, Kang was carrying his weapon on his body, though he hadn't yet thought there was a need to draw it. He reached for the doorknob and twisted as he moved forward, but instead of running through an open door, he crashed directly into it. He had mistimed the opening. Unnecessary time wasted.

He twisted the doorknob once more and pushed forward. The door flew open, revealing the narrow hallway leading to the front of the house. The light from the kitchen spilled into the dark hallway, revealing the doorway opposite the kitchen—the guestroom where Xiaolian had stayed.

Kang charged past Po Po's room, still unaware why Abby had screamed, but he knew he had to keep moving. Straight ahead he had a limited view of the living room. The front door was off to the right side, just out of his view. He could tell it was open, as the sun hadn't completely set and the natural light spilled onto the wooden floors.

"No! Don't do it." I pleaded as I moved in closer.

He showed no sign of comprehending what I was saying, but I knew he understood me. He still had that wry grin on his face. He was enjoying every second.

I was feet away and closing in. Thoughts of what my next move would be filled my head.

Go for the gun?

Tackle Lucy out of the way?

Tackle him and worry about the gun later?

No matter what I thought of, none of the options jumped out to me as the right choice. But I had to make a decision, fast.

The gun. Go for his gun and put yourself between it and Lucy.

That was my decision. I committed to it. My focus narrowed. I knew what I had to do to save my daughter.

His smile widened.

His shoulders bounced slightly.

I couldn't for the life of me understand why he was laughing until the obvious dawned on me.

My steps.

What's happening?

The rubber sole of the cross-trainers I wore had a firm grip on the area rug, becoming entangled. My torso moved forward, but my legs remained in a battle of their own with my feet. A tear streamed down my cheek.

No, Abby. Don't fall. Recover. You can do it.

But as hard as I tried, I could not correct the course of my movements. The pull was too great. The battle with gravity was lost.

I crashed onto the floor before reaching up with one hand, toward him. My eyesight already marred by the welling of tears. "Not her," I pleaded.

It was all I could do. I had to hope he would take mercy on me and change his mind. If he had to take someone from my family, if there was no changing the outcome of him pulling the trigger, then at least spare Lucy.

"Take me," I shouted. "TAKE ME!"

CHAPTER FIFTY-NINE

THE RAYS of the sun sparkled across the calm waters of the bay as sailboats cut across. Up above, blue skies stretched for miles without a single fluffy cloud daring to mar its façade.

Reilly drove the SUV. Kang sat in the front passenger seat, and House sat in the backseat. They had just picked her up from the Bureau's satellite office in Oakland and were driving to a facility in Silicone Valley. As they drove across the Bay Bridge, Kang stared lazily out of the window at nothing in particular. His thoughts were on the events that had taken place a few days ago. In fact, it was all he thought of.

Over and over he would replay that afternoon at Abby's house. He had been sitting comfortably in a lawn chair, sipping his beer. Abby sat next to him. Ryan stood a few feet away, showing off some of his judo moves. "Uncle Kyle, do you want to see something I learned with my nunchucks?" Reilly and House were laughing over a story he was telling her. Sokolov and Bennie were still picking at a rack of ribs while Green told them about being raised in a hippie commune. Po Po was busy trying to feed people more food. Lucy sang out loud as she walked from group to group.

A great bunch of people had gathered that day to celebrate his one-year anniversary with the FBI. He was glad Abby had gone through the trouble of pulling the party together, even after his insistence that he wasn't interested. She knew him better than he knew himself.

"We need more ice," he remembered her saying before heading inside. He'd watched Lucy run after her, with Ryan right behind them.

He'd been staring at the sky, draining the last of his beer when he heard it, the scream from inside the house. He remembered quickly scanning the backyard to see if anyone else had heard it. But it was business as usual.

He knew he hadn't imagined it. He didn't question it. He knew that much. He stood fast, flipping the lawn chair over in the process. That was the first that anybody else realized something might be wrong. But the concern wasn't with the scream from inside the house; it was with him.

He remembered House calling his name, and him not answering. He'd known that he hadn't the time to spare.

Reaching out for the doorknob, twisting it open and mistiming the door opening. *Idiot. Rookie move.* He couldn't get over that it had even happened.

A few seconds lost there.

Running down the hall had posed no problem. He couldn't have done it any differently. Or could he have? He could have had used that time to draw his weapon. But why would he? As terrifying as that scream had sounded, was it cause enough to reach for his gun?

When he finally did reach the living room, it had taken a

moment or two to comprehend what was happening. Had he lost time there?

Kang had logged over fifteen years with SFPD before becoming an FBI. He had more than enough experience in the field to assess a situation quickly and react.

Had he unnecessarily taken an extra moment? Had reaching for his gun a beat later cost him time he didn't have to spare? Did it matter? No, it didn't, because what happened next was what really had cost him time.

His hand had slipped off the butt of his gun.

It had never happened before. He had practiced drawing his gun at least a thousand times over his career. So why had his hand slipped that day? Same gun. Same holster. Had he simply choked? Was what he'd seen unfolding before his eyes been enough to throw him off his game?

Perhaps.

Not only did he have to make a second attempt at drawing his weapon, he pulled forward too early. The barrel hadn't cleared the holster and because of that, it twisted out of his grasp. The realization that he had just lost complete control of his weapon, that it was falling to the floor, that he would have to once again grab hold of it, that it could even take a nasty bounce away from him... it was unrelenting.

The utter hopelessness he had felt as he looked at his partner, lying on the floor, screaming at an armed man standing in the doorway. Two of them, veterans of law enforcement, and yet neither capable of doing what years of training had prepared them for.

The gunshot echoed off the walls. A single shot. That was all that was needed.

Had he failed that day? In his mind he had. Little Lucy, a

person he cared a great deal for, had needed his help more than
ever and he had not delivered.

But someone had.

———

Ryan didn't freeze when he looked out the second-floor window
and spotted a man with his shirt collar torn and what appeared
to be blood splattered on his face walking up the pathway to
their front door. He wasted no time calling for help and waiting
for someone else to do something.

He reacted.

Pivoting on the balls of his feet, he sprinted to his mother's
bedroom at the end of the hall. Timing was everything. He
knew where Abby kept her weapon. He knew how to lock the
clip into place without fumbling, without having to think it
through. He knew how to grip the weapon tightly with both
hands. He knew how to switch the safety off. And he did it all
seamlessly.

He hurried down the stairs, knowing full well his next move
wasn't to find his mother and give her the gun. The scream he
had heard earlier told him everything he had to know.

He watched Kang run past the bottom of the steps, but
seeing him didn't lessen his resolve. It didn't slow him. It didn't
cause him to rethink the action he was about to take. If he had
done any one of those things, the events of that day would have
unfolded differently.

As soon as Ryan had a clear view of the front door, he
planted his feet firmly on the steps the best he could. He raised
the handgun, drew a breath, took aim, and did exactly what he

had seen his mother do time and time again. Protect people from the bad guys.

CHAPTER SIXTY

The black SUV exited Highway 101 at the North Shoreline off ramp and then continued west on Stierlin Road toward the mountains west of the city of Mountain View. Their destination was a secured government complex. Neither Reilly, Kang, nor House had been there before. In fact, all three of them had required the Department of Justice to issue them the appropriate security clearance.

House hadn't said anything more than a simple hello since climbing into the backseat of the SUV. She was content to be alone in her thoughts, not that Reilly or Kang were bothered by it. The radio was tuned to a jazz station; anything more than that would have disturbed the tranquil state of the vehicle.

House had been friends with Abby for quite some time. She still remembered the day she met the feisty woman, who had a mouth with a mind of its own. Nothing filtered. All raw. She had liked her immediately.

When House had seen Kang pop out of his lawn chair like a kernel of corn in a hot pan, she knew something was wrong. She hadn't heard the scream; at the time, Reilly was doing his impression of his uncle's duck call.

She'd hesitated though. It wasn't long. Still she couldn't understand why. She'd seen the look on Kang's face, and yet she'd questioned her instincts, thinking she was reading it wrong. They were at a BBQ. Everyone was having a great time. Why would there be trouble?

House had bolted past Reilly, after Kang. She heard him curse as he slammed into the door leading into the house. She had pulled open the screen door of the porch just as he entered the house.

As she chased after him, her eyes settled on his right hand. It looked as if he was contemplating drawing his weapon. *Does he see something that I don't?* This alone had House moving her hand to her right hip.

She heard the second scream and drew her weapon.

Kang came to a stop just after the bottom of the stairs, half of his body dipped out of view—the half that would have told her if he had drawn his weapon.

Then the loud crack of a gun being discharged had echoed throughout the house. Someone had fired. Was it Kang? Was it Abby?

House had raised her handgun, allowing it to lead the way as she came up behind Kang. *Move to his left. Get around him and assess*, she had thought as she began to side step, her eyes trained down the barrel of her gun.

Kang was reaching for his weapon, which was on the floor. He hadn't fired. Lucy stood by the door, crying. A strange man lay motionless on the floor next to her. A few feet away was Abby. She lay prone, slightly on her side.

House had quickly holstered her gun and hurried over to Abby with one thought on her mind.

Stop.

The.

Bleeding.

Reilly brought the SUV to a stop at the intersection. He checked his watch; it was fifteen minutes to ten. Traffic over the bridge was light, and he expected they would arrive for their appointment on time. He inhaled deeply and then let out an airy breath through his mouth. *One minute we're enjoying a BBQ, and the next my team and I are en route to a government facility I had no idea existed before today.*

The light turned green, and Reilly stepped on the gas pedal. He glanced once more at the GPS console to ensure they were still heading in the right direction. They were. He knew it. Still he glanced at it again. It wasn't a nervous tic. More like an uncomfortable one. He still hadn't come to grips with his actions.

That day at Abby's place, he was the third person to arrive at the terrible scene in the living room. Earlier he had been in the middle of making a stupid duck sound when House disappeared.

He'd spun around, "It's that bad?" he had said, laughing.

At that point, he was still unaware of the deadly situation unfolding. He tried to tell himself that he hadn't been the only one who was clueless. Sokolov, Bennie, and Green were still conversing, though Sokolov had craned his neck at House's abrupt exit.

No matter how Reilly tried to spin his actions in those first few moments, he couldn't deny it. He'd screwed up. His instincts were off. Chalk it up to not being in the field and spending most of his time behind a desk.

Still, Reilly always thought he could react appropriately when needed. He never once thought his training had been compromised. And really it hadn't. Tactically, Reilly had done nothing wrong; he'd arrived in the living room only a few seconds after House. Yes, the situation had been defused by then, but someone had to be first, someone had to be second, and someone had to be the third to arrive.

When he got there, Kang had Lucy in his arms. A man lay unconscious next to them. House was on the floor with Abby's head cradled in her arms and resting in her lap. She was applying pressure to Abby's neck.

Reilly was already on his phone calling for an ambulance when he noticed Ryan standing on the stairs, still holding the handgun in his trembling hands. Tears trailed down his face, but he wasn't sobbing. He just stared ahead.

Reilly had reached out slowly and taken hold of the firearm. "Let go, son," he remembered telling him before giving the boy a hug. But the truth was... he didn't know the severity of Abby's injury. It was unquestionable that the amount of blood he'd seen wasn't a healthy sign, but she did appear to be conscious, as he'd seen House whisper in her ear.

Reilly made a left onto a quiet lane that deadended at the foot of the mountains. Straight ahead he saw a lift gate with a small guardhouse off to the side. He slowed the vehicle, and a uniformed military guard appeared. Reilly gave him their names, and after a quick check, he was waved through. The lift

gate rose and the ground barrier lowered itself, allowing the
SUV to drive onward. Reilly followed the map the guard had
given him to Building D.

Inside the small lobby, another guard manning a counter
asked for credentials and checked the system. He told them to
have a seat and wait. A few minutes later, two men—one
wearing a navy-blue suit, the other a white lab coat—appeared.

"Special Agent Reilly, did you have trouble finding the
place?" the man in the suit asked.

"The directions were spot-on," Reilly responded. "This is
Agent Kang and Agent House."

The man in the suit extended his arm. "It's a pleasure to
meet you. My name is Gerald Watkins, and I'm the director
here. This man standing next to me is Dr. Julian Yates."

With the introductions complete, Watkins led the group
down a tile-floor hall. There were no pictures on the walls, no
notices, no signs. They walked through a series of double doors,
each one requiring Watkins to use his security card to gain
entrance. They didn't pass a single person the entire time.

Eventually they reached a hall lined with gray doors. Each
one had a viewing window.

"She's in room F," Watkins said as he pointed at the door.

Reilly stepped forward and peeked through the glass pane.
Lying on the bed with her arms and legs secured by restraints
was Xiaolian.

"She's sleeping," Dr. Yates said. "We keep her restrained
because she's been having vivid nightmares and we don't want
her hurting herself. Aside from that, she's doing fine health-
wise."

Kang and House each took a peek at the girl.

Xiaolian had turned up at Abby's house shortly after the shooting—out of breath, sweat pouring off every inch of her body. She had run most of the way from the motel to Abby's home. She froze when she saw the person lying in the doorway. And it was through her that Reilly learned about Walter Chan, the twin brother to Alonzo Chan, the man they still hadn't identified.

Once she had calmed, she was able to fill Reilly in on what had happened to her and the man who had taken her. A team of agents dispatched to the motel confirmed her story. In the room, they'd found him dead.

It wasn't until she began to talk about where she was from that red flags were raised. A mysterious home in an undisclosed location, experiments and testing, the fact that her real name was Abby. It was a story fit for science fiction. Reilly had no choice but to elevate the matter. It was beyond him.

Once the DOJ got involved, they took over the investigation, quarantined the girl, and advised Reilly and his team not to mention a single word about her to anyone. If the Chinese were indeed behind this, the State Department had a keen interest in why they were meddling in something far worse than cloning.

"How long do you expect to keep her here?" Reilly asked.

Watkins referred the question to Dr. Yates. "That's a hard question to answer," Yates said. "We've just started our testing. We still need to debrief her and confirm everything you've told us. I would say the answer is indefinitely." Yates noticed Kang looking through the viewing window of another door. "You can go inside if you want. It's fine."

Kang reached for the knob and turned it. He pushed the door open and walked into the small room. It was sparse, just a bed and tray stand holding a pitcher of water and a plastic cup.

The walls were painted white, as was the ceiling, and the floor was the same white tile as in the hallway.

Yates came up behind Kang. "The restraints are temporary. Procedure."

He nodded. "How is she?"

"Agent Kane is fine, for now."

THE END.

That concludes book one in the Suitcase Girl trilogy. In book two, The Curator, the government directs Abby to find the truth behind the mysterious girl. Is she a national threat? But there are others who are determined to prevent this from happening. For a preview, turn the page.

THE
CUR
ATOR

ABBY KANE THRILLER

TY HUTCHINSON

AN EXCERPT FROM THE CURATOR
BOOK 2, SG TRILOGY - ABBY KANE FBI THRILLER #8

A man stood slightly hunched over and leaning against the trunk of a pine tree, uncertain of his next step. With each exhale, his breaths billowed in smoky plumes across his chattering teeth. His eyes shifted erratically from side to side.

Where am I?

He had just taken two steps away from the security of the tree, his bare feet sinking into mossy dirt, when the crack of a branch jerked his head to the left.

What was that?

He squinted and scanned the misty woods, carefully moving forward and nearly tripping over his own steps at the sudden appearance of a mountain bike flying right past him. It landed a few feet away, its back wheel kicking up dirt.

"The crazies are out early today," the rider spouted off as he pedaled hard, disappearing into the maze of trees as quickly as he had appeared.

The man looked down at himself. A tattered hospital gown hung from his bony frame. He gripped it and tugged. A rip formed near the shoulder. He grabbed the thin fabric with his other hand and yanked. The gown fell away from him, exposing his pale nakedness.

Aside from his breathing, the woods were eerily quiet. There were no birds singing or breezes rustling the tree branches. He walked in the direction the mountain biker had disappeared.

Am I dreaming? Maybe I am. God, I hope so.

The situation was surreal; it had to be. He hoped it was, for the last thing he remembered was puffing on a cigar and sipping scotch. There was a warm glow of a fireplace, and he wasn't alone. Others were gathered around him. It felt like he knew them, but he couldn't be sure. His memory was nothing more than spotty imagery.

He struggled to find clarity, something that could begin to explain the oddness of his predicament. The harder he tried to recall, the more confused he became. Random people and places popped into his head, but they meant nothing. He couldn't remember his name or what he did for living.

Do I even work?

He continued down the side of the mountain, his body warming from the physical movement. Perspiration appeared, creating a slickness across his skin.

Picking up speed, he tripped over an exposed tree root, nearly falling flat on his face. In fact, his balance seemed off kilter ever since... well, he couldn't remember. A filmy substance in his eyes marred his vision, which he couldn't clear no matter how much he blinked or wiped at them. But he remained focused as best he could and pushed forward. All he wanted was to go home, wherever that was, and climb into bed.

A clearing in the trees up ahead revealed the tops of buildings—a skyline with a large bay behind it.

I hope this is where I live.

It seemed slightly familiar to his gut. But if he did live in this city, he had no clue as to where.

I'll just ask for help. Someone will offer it.

He kept his pace, skirting trees and bushes along the way.

Almost there, keep going.

The sounds of urbanization began to fill the quiet void: a blaring horn, a barking dog, the engine of a large vehicle shifting gears. With each step, the city revealed more and more of itself.

Just as he'd walked out of the woods and onto a sidewalk, a loud shriek filled his ears.

He looked in that direction and spotted a woman pulling her child close to her as she backed away, while a couple carrying coffees stopped in their tracks. They all had horrified expressions on their faces.

Wait, what's wrong?

Vehicles slowed as drivers and passengers pointed and stared.

Why won't anyone help me? Sir, could you call an ambulance? I'm not well.

A man walking his dog shouted at him. "Back off, buddy!"

What's wrong with these people? I'm just asking for help.

A siren could be heard, coming closer.

Finally, someone heard me.

A police vehicle screeched to a stop along the curb. The doors flew open, and two officers exited with weapons drawn. "Stop right there."

Is that really necessary? I just need help.

One of them advanced on him. "Get down on your knees now, or I'm tasing you."

Tase me?

"I'm not telling you again. Get down now!"

Before the man could comprehend the situation, an intense explosion of pain ripped throughout his body, causing him to collapse onto the sidewalk. His body clenched into a withering ball, and his eyes rolled back into his head as he struggled to breathe.

I just need help.

Get your copy now.

A NOTE FROM TY HUTCHINSON

Thank you for reading SUITCASE GIRL. If you're a fan of Abby, spread the word to friends, family, book clubs, and reader groups online. You can also help get the word out by leaving a review.

Visit my website to sign up for my Spam-Free Newsletter and receive "First Look" content, and information about future releases, promotions, and giveaways. I promise never to spam. I can't stand receiving it myself. With that said, I've made it really easy to unsubscribe at any time.

I love hearing from readers. Let's connect.
www.tyhutchinson.com
tyhutchinson@tyhutchinson.com

Contract: Wolf Den

Contract: Endgame

Mui Thrillers

A Book of Truths

A Book of Vengeance

A Book of Revelations

A Book of Villains

Mui Action Thrillers

The Monastery

The Blood Grove

The Minotaur

Darby Stansfield Thrillers

The Accidental Criminal

(previously titled Chop Suey)

The Russian Problem

(previously titled Stroganov)

Holiday With A P.I.

(previously titled Loco Moco)

Other Thrilling Reads

Published by Ty Hutchinson

Copyright © 2017 by Ty Hutchinson

Cover Art: Damonza

Printed in Great Britain
by Amazon

80940431R00202